A Girl Called Problem

A Girl Called Problem

by
Katie Quirk

Eerdmans Books for Young Readers
Grand Rapids, Michigan • Cambridge, U.K.

Text © 2013 Katie Quirk

Published 2013 by Eerdmans Books for Young Readers,
an imprint of Wm. B. Eerdmans Publishing Co.
2140 Oak Industrial Dr. NE, Grand Rapids, Michigan 49505
P.O. Box 163, Cambridge CB3 9PU U.K.

www.eerdmans.com/youngreaders

15 16 17 18   8 7 6 5 4 3 2

Library of Congress Cataloging-in-Publication Data

Quirk, Katie.
A girl called Problem / by Katie Quirk.
p. cm.
Summary: In 1967 Tanzania, when President Nyerere urges his people
to work together as one extended family, the people of Litongo move to
a new village which, to some, seems cursed, but where thirteen-year-old
Shida, a healer, sees hope for the future when she not only gets to study
with a nurse she admires, but she and her female cousins are allowed to
attend school. Includes glossary and author's note.
ISBN 978-0-8028-5404-9
1. Tanzania — History — 1964 — Juvenile fiction. [1. Tanzania —
History — 1964 — Fiction. 2. Villages — Fiction. 3. Sukuma (African
people) — Fiction. 4. Healers — Fiction. 5. Moving, Household —
Fiction. 6. Mothers and daughters — Fiction. 7. Blessing and cursing —
Fiction. 8. Farm life — Tanzania — Fiction.] I. Title.
PZ7.Q478Gir 2013
[Fic] — dc23
2012025468

Cover illustration © 2013 Richard Tuschman

For Modesta

Chapter 1

Village of Litongo
Tanzania, East Africa
1967

Great fires erupt from tiny sparks.
— *Libyan proverb*

Tum, tum, tum, ratta, tum, tum, tum. The village's talking drums cut through the humid air. From as far away as the base of the distant hills, the people of Litongo hurried toward the drums, across the rocky landscape and through fields of cotton, rice, and maize. Cowherd boys whacked their animals' rumps, corralling them early for the day. Women in bright head wraps, collecting water at the river, abandoned their buckets and ran in the direction of the thunderous beat.

In the village of Litongo, people knew that drums had souls. When drummers hit the tightly-strung leather, the instruments spoke. Sometimes the drums announced a death, and sometimes their rhythm goaded dancers to throw their legs and arms higher into the air, but today they were announcing a meeting, an important meeting. The elders of Litongo had been consulting in private for nearly two days. Whispers were floating around that the elders were considering moving the entire village, but no one really believed the rumor. The people of Litongo had lived in this place for generations, and moving the village made as much sense as moving the moon.

In the compound where the village drummers played stood two thatched mud huts, a circular cattle corral made of stacked thorny brambles, and a large mango tree. Not far from the tree, a line of elders and a young woman dressed all in white sat on stools and cowhide chairs. A girl crouched on a branch of the mango tree.

None of the elders in the yard noticed the girl in the tree. Her skin was a beautiful dark brown that blended in with the shadows of the mango tree, and her once-yellow dress was now stained and faded to the color of the earth. The girl reached up with a muscular arm and grabbed a mango from the branch just above her head. She took a knife from the leather pouch tied around her waist and cut into the plump fruit. Juice gushed onto the skirt of her dress. She swung her hands out to let the drippings fall to the ground, but as her eyes followed the juice down, she jerked the mango back.

The long, lean face of another girl squinted up at the girl in the tree. The girl below wiped mango juice off her mat of short, black hair and glared up into the branches with enormous brown eyes. "Shida!" she said. "I guess you were given the right name, after all."

Shida meant "problem" in Swahili. The villagers of Litongo spoke the tribal language of Sukuma, and though some of them had never learned their new national language, Swahili, everyone knew what the name Shida meant. A family that had been cursed around the time of a child's birth named their baby Shida to mark the curse.

Normally, Shida got angry when people teased her about her name, but seeing her serious cousin Grace glaring up at her, all she could do was laugh. "Oh, come on, Grace. It was an accident." Shida swung her legs, causing the mangoes and leaves around her to quiver. While Grace was tall and elegant like a giraffe, Shida was short and strong, packed with springy spunk, like a Thomson's gazelle. She had a radiant smile and big, round cheeks that showed off her perfect white teeth. "Come up here. We've got so much to talk about."

"I can't come up there, Shida," Grace said. She placed her lanky hands on her hips and frowned up at her cousin. "You know I'll get scolded. Young women aren't supposed to climb trees."

Shida sighed and flopped her short body down to rest

on the tree branch. Grace took everything so seriously, especially villagers' comments about the two of them becoming young women. According to the adults who kept reprimanding Shida, she and Grace, both thirteen, shouldn't be scrambling up trees to cut branches for firewood. They shouldn't be running to the other side of the village to deliver messages. Instead, they should stay at their mothers' sides, training to be good wives and perfecting their cooking, rice pounding, and farming. In fact, Shida's mother had recently mentioned finding a husband for her daughter. But if marriage was anything like it had been for her mother, Shida was pretty sure she wasn't interested.

Shida swung down from the tree, dropping into a squat right next to Grace. She tugged at the body of her yellow dress, trying to stretch the strained material where it squeezed her growing chest, and gripped her cousin's arm. "Climb up there with me, Grace." She looked over her shoulder and lowered her voice. "People say the elders are going to move all of Litongo."

Grace raised one eyebrow. "Move Litongo? You know that's impossible, Shida. We've never even visited another village. Why would the elders want us to move?"

"Well of course it's impossible," Shida said. "But whatever the elders are going to tell us, the nurse is over there and you have to come up in this tree and get a good look at her. Oh, Grace, she's so beautiful."

Grace peeked over her shoulder at the crowd gathering in the yard. Everyone was busy talking or staring at the elders and the nurse. No one was looking at the two girls. "Alright, but only this once." Grace shimmied up the trunk, her bony knees and elbows poking out at odd angles.

"I heard you were at Mama Nganza's hut last night," Grace said after Shida had stepped around her and settled farther out on the branch. "Was she sick?"

"*Mmmhmm*," Shida answered, distracted. She fingered the pouch of medicinal leaves, roots, and tree bark she always tied to her waist. People said Shida had the touch of a healer, and when women like Mama Nganza couldn't afford to call one of the village's two medicine men to cure an illness in their family, they sometimes asked Shida for help.

But Shida wasn't thinking about Mama Nganza right now. She was staring down at the nurse, whose white dress and square white hat made a striking contrast to her dark skin. "How do you think she keeps her clothes so white? Is the river water in Njia Panda cleaner than here?"

Grace turned and squinted at her cousin. "Who are you talking about, Shida? Mama Nganza? She's never been to Njia Panda."

Njia Panda was the distant village over the hills that loomed on the horizon. The nurse lived in Njia Panda and for the past few months, usually around the full moon, she made the long journey to Litongo to provide medicine to those who were feeling sick. Though many of the villagers were wary of the nurse's funny white pills, they were proud of her visits. She was sent by Tanzania's first and much-adored president, Julius Nyerere. People thought of Nyerere almost as a god. Shida's aunt, Mama Kulwa, even had a *kitenge* cloth printed with Nyerere's handsome face. Nyerere had helped free Tanzania from the *wazungu*, the white colonizers, and now villagers said he was trying to help them build the best country in all of Africa. As far as everyone in Litongo was concerned, if the nurse was sent by Nyerere, then she had to be good.

But for Shida, the nurse was more than good — she was a dream come true. Shida didn't have anyone in Litongo who could teach her about being a healer. Some of the old women in the village told her about one plant or another, but each of them only knew how to cure a few sicknesses. The village medicine men were knowledgable, but they dealt mostly in curses and none of them would take on a girl apprentice. Every time the nurse came to Litongo, Shida hovered next to her and studied her every move. On one occasion she had even faked a fever in order to try out the nurse's tiny pills.

Ta, tum, tum, tum.

As if controlled by some powerful magic, the crowd grew silent and stepped back a few feet to give space to the elders. All eyes turned to Babu, Shida and Grace's grand-father, on whose compound the villagers were gathered. Although Litongo didn't have a chief, everyone considered Babu the most respected elder.

Shida and Grace could only see the back of Babu's head with his black, curly hair, which had grown slightly dusted with gray in the last few years. Instead of his usual thin white T-shirt, Babu wore his fancy purple batik shirt. Shida smiled. Even from the back, Babu looked gentle and kind.

"President Nyerere, the father of our nation, has sent an important message, my children," Babu said.

Shida pictured their handsome president whose image, pinned to a wall of Babu's hut, she stared at nearly every day.

"Now that we are an independent country, Nyerere wants all of us to have education and medical dispensaries. He says that we must learn and be healthy in order to be strong, independent Africans."

The elders in the crowd hummed in agreement.

Shida was used to Babu's slow way of talking. She spent most evenings, after she had finished cooking and cleaning, sitting next to Babu on his second cowhide chair outside the old man's hut. But today Shida leaned forward like everyone in the crowd. What had the elders been meeting about? If Nyerere wanted all of them to be educated and have medical dispensaries, then maybe Litongo would be given a school. Maybe the nurse would even move to their village to set up a clinic. Shida hiccupped, as she often did when she was excited, and covered her mouth.

Several heads down below turned to look up at her. One of them was the scowling face of her mother, Mama Shida. Mama Shida was slumped against their mud hut, her matted hair sticking out in wild tufts and her skin a sooty gray from months of being unoiled. Her two rectangles of faded red *kitenge* cloth, which she wrapped around her waist and torso, were tattered and dirty. Like all Sukuma mothers, Mama was named after her first child, and right now she looked just like her name: Mama Shida, Mother of Problems.

"In order to live like true Africans," Babu continued, "President Nyerere says we must live closer. We must have many of us together like trees in a forest, so that we can share one school and one dispensary and many other things. And that means that many of us must move." Babu did not pause this time. "President Nyerere has asked that those of us living in Litongo move to the village of Njia Panda, where we will be provided a dispensary and a school and where we will join that village as one."

The sea of yellow, green, and red cloth-wrapped heads, cornrow braids, and straw hats seethed forward. Murmurs thundered through the yard. Shida had to clutch the branch below her for fear of falling. Move from Litongo to

Njia Panda? But that was impossible.

"My children," Babu said. "I know you'll have many questions, but first let me introduce our guest here, Nurse Goldfilda. She's been living in Njia Panda since the last heavy monsoon rain and she can explain more about this new village."

The nurse stood up, half facing the crowd and half facing Babu. Her hand ran up and down the buttons that lined the front of her starched white dress. "Greetings, my fellow countrymen. What is your news?"

A dog barked in the distance, but otherwise the yard was quiet. The nervous rumbling in Shida's stomach grew as she watched the nurse. Why hadn't Babu given the nurse a translator? The nurse only spoke Swahili, not Sukuma.

The nurse looked back at Babu and he nodded to a man in the crowd, his youngest son, Shida's uncle Magema.

Magema stood and cleared his throat. "The nurse . . ." Magema's voice cracked. "The nurse here says hello and asks what our news is."

Babu nodded at the crowd. Tanzanians always greeted each other by asking for their neighbors' news, and they always answered positively, even if someone in their family had recently died.

"Peaceful," a few villagers replied.

Nurse Goldfilda's mouth twitched with a nervous smile. "Good. As our elder here has explained, President Nyerere wants us to live in *ujamaa* villages so that we can work together and share services that we all need. Our president sent me to Njia Panda four months ago to help start up a medical clinic, and now he's asking that your village move to Njia Panda to share the clinic and school and farmland."

"But we can't move!" one man said. He was leaning on a *jembe* hoe near the front of the crowd. "Everything we need is right here and, anyway, who would we send to this school you speak of?"

"Well . . ." Nurse Goldfilda continued to fiddle with the buttons on the front of her dress. She normally appeared almost regal with her thick cornrow braids lining her skull, her perfect white leather shoes, and her plump body that showed she had plenty of good food to eat. But today, she looked like Shida felt when she was being scolded by Mama.

"Well, sir, all of the children could go to school, girls and boys, young and old, all of them. I know this would be difficult at first. You'd have fewer hands to help you in the fields, but they'd learn how to write and read and work with numbers — skills that would help them be better farmers, or even have other jobs when they are older."

"Us go to school!" Shida mouthed the words to her cousin, and Grace smiled back, wide-eyed.

"Girls!" Grumpy old Mzee Kalanga didn't even wait for Uncle Magema to translate what the nurse said. "Well, you must know what I think of girls going to school. But for the boys, what are these other jobs you speak of?"

"Some of them . . ." The nurse cleared her throat. "Some of the children, if they were interested, could become teachers for our school, textile mill workers in our nation's cities, engineers for our rail system, or even nurses like me." She turned to the mango tree and her eyes met Shida's through the spaces between the thick green leaves.

Shida hiccupped.

"Like this girl in the tree. Sh . . ." The nurse paused for a moment as if she were second-guessing Shida's name. "Shida," she said. "She seems interested in healing. Whenever I come to Litongo, Shida sits with me and already she's learned something about my ways of doing medicine. If she went to school and worked with me, she could be the next nurse of Njia Panda."

The next nurse of Njia Panda! This time Shida felt Grace's hands brace her waist to keep her from falling out of the tree.

"Who are these villagers who live in Njia Panda?" Uncle Magema finished his translation and went straight into asking a question. "Are they Sukuma like us, or are they of another tribe, like you?"

"The people of Njia Panda are Sukuma, like you," the nurse said. "You'd build your homes and fields to the side of their village. The two schoolteachers and I are the only non-Sukuma in Njia Panda, but your children would learn to speak Swahili in the schools in order to communicate with us and all of the tribes of Tanzania. President Nyerere says in order for us to be a true African nation, we must look beyond our tribes and all speak one shared African language, not English or French as the *wazungu* had us do."

"But we can't abandon everything," old Mzee Kalanga said. "What would become of our houses and fields here in Litongo? What about our traditions?"

"You'd leave these compounds behind," the nurse said. "The government has promised you new land and even supplies to build new homes in Njia Panda. But you'd certainly bring your traditions with you — President Nyerere is not asking you to leave behind your Sukuma ways. He is asking you to remain Sukuma and to come lead."

Shida closed her eyes, hoping to calm her excited thoughts. Njia Panda. What could it possibly be like? Uncle Bujiko and the few other villagers who had been there only complained of the arduous day-long journey over the mountains. Was there a river there? What did the people wear? Did they eat rice and corn porridge *ugali,* or some foreign food?

"Forgive me, Father, but I see no reason why we should move." The compound nearly rumbled with the thunderous voice of Grace's father, Uncle Bujiko. He stood at the front of the crowd with his shoulders turned to face Babu, not the nurse.

Grace sighed, and Shida put her hand on top of her cousin's.

"In Njia Panda," Uncle Bujiko said, "the villagers may be Sukuma, but these government workers who are not of our tribe, how can they help us? We already have learning and healing, Father. The children learn the ways of our people from their parents, and their grandparents prepare them to be good husbands and wives. We're healthy, and when the ancestors don't give us good health, we have our medicine men to help us. Besides, some of us have been to this Njia Panda and have seen how they live all crowded together. We Sukuma like our space, spread out across large fields and distant compounds. With all due respect, Father, I don't believe Njia Panda is for us."

Shida glared at her uncle. Of course he, a rich man with many cattle and huge cotton fields, wouldn't want to move to Njia Panda. But Shida's gaze drifted to Babu, who was stamping his walking stick in the dirt in front of him, trying to push himself up. With the third stamp, he hefted himself onto his feet and stumbled forward to gain his balance. "We understand your fears, my child." He shuffled in a half circle to look at the rest of the crowd. "As all of you know, we elders have carefully discussed this question of moving. None of us would have considered leaving Litongo before. Moving means abandoning our fields where we've worked so hard, leaving our huts, our rocks, and our hills whose shapes and bumps we've memorized like those of our own bodies.

"But as the nurse says, we're being called as villagers, as Sukuma, to come and lead this nation. Never before have we been able to count ourselves as part of an independent African nation. Never before have we had a president who comes from among us. The *wazungu* who once ruled this country had us fight in their wars, but the wars ended and we returned to Litongo. Some of us left to work on the *wazungu's* railroad, but even for that we would not permanently leave Litongo. Other independent African nations, our very own neighbors, are ruled by rich African men who prefer speaking in the languages of the *wazungu*, driving these boxes they call motor cars, and growing fat with money from factories. If such men ruled our country and asked us to move, we would not leave Litongo. Not for them.

"But President Nyerere is asking us to move for something that has never been done before. He is asking us to build *ujamaa*, African familyhood. He is looking to villagers like us, peasants, and he is saying ours is the way worth living. He wants all Tanzanians to come together, to work harder than we ever have before, farming the land and growing our knowledge. He says that we should build our nation not out of factories and motor cars, fancy roads and electric lights, but out of villages and plows, and peasants who know how to read and write and care for all people, girls and boys, men and women, old and young. He says we should live as Africans did before the *wazungu* came, as an extended family. President Nyerere is asking us to lead a revolution. None of us has ever been asked to lead a revolution. For that we are willing to leave Litongo."

Shida felt a shiver run up her spine. The churning in her stomach had turned to a flutter.

"So you elders have decided, Babu?" A young man's voice pierced the silence just as a rooster crowed in the neighboring compound.

"Some have decided to stay," Babu said. "Our old medicine man, the *mganga*, is tired." Babu pointed to the frail man sitting next to him. "He's been here for more cycles of rain and sun than the rest of us can imagine. He's decided to stay with a few of his sons. None of us can pretend this move will be easy, and so three other families have decided to stay behind as well.

"The rest of us, however, including the young medicine man . . ." Babu paused and took a long, labored breath, as if he were working to lift something into the air above his chest. "The rest of us have decided to take our families to Njia Panda."

The yard below erupted in sound. Shida looked down at her hand, realizing it was still clamped onto Grace's.

"Grace, this is good, no?"

Grace sat tall and stiff on the branch like a maize stock, her eyes wide in shock. "I . . . I . . ." she stuttered.

Shida stood up on the branch, knocking her head on leaves and unripe mango fruit. She shimmied over to Grace, bracing herself on one of her cousin's shoulders. "Grace, this really will be good. We won't have to farm all day. We'll get to go to school and the nurse will —"

"Shida, get down here!"

Shida seized up at the sound of Mama's raspy voice coming from the base of the tree. She slid down the trunk and was met with her mother's eyes bulging out and her mouth hanging open. Mama looked like she had a year ago when Mzee Kalanga's dog attacked her.

"Haven't we had enough bad fortune?" Mama stared off at the horizon in the opposite direction of the hills.

Shida put her hands on her mother's wiry shoulders. "Mama, we can trust Babu. He wouldn't make us leave Litongo if it were going to bring us harm."

Mama's eyes shot back at Shida. "How can you be so sure? You know our family's cursed. You know why you were given your name. When Babu sent me away from this village, the curse began, and when I brought you back to Litongo, I vowed never to leave again."

Shida studied her mother's face. Mama had *vowed* never to leave Litongo? Sukuma people didn't make vows lightly.

They knew that the world was much bigger than what they saw right in front of them. Ancestors were there in the air and the water and the trees. Their spirits wrapped in and around the old Sukuma stories Shida and her mother told at night. When people in the village died or crops failed, it was always because some ancestor was unhappy. Surely, the ancestors would punish Mama if she broke such a vow.

"Mama . . ." Shida tried to keep her hands steady on her mother's shoulders. "Mama, you couldn't have made a vow about leaving Litongo. You probably just —"

"Go cook dinner, Shida." Mama gritted her teeth, releasing each word like a blow of the pestle into their rice-pounding mortar.

"I'll go, Mama," Shida said. She turned to run to their kitchen hut, but Shida found herself glancing over her shoulder, as if misfortune were already stalking her. What if Mama was right? What if they left Litongo, only to learn they'd been cursed?

Chapter 2

She who hates, hates herself.
— South African proverb

Crouching over a wood fire in their cramped, clay-walled cooking hut, Shida leaned back on her heels, rolled her head, and felt her stiff neck pop. For the last hour as the crowd dispersed from their compound, she had run out to collect firewood from the forest and carried it back in a huge bundle on her head. At first, Shida had been annoyed at Mama for failing to collect wood earlier that day — Mama had promised she would. But chopping trees with her machete had allowed Shida extra time to sift through her many questions about leaving Litongo.

Shida balanced a pot of water on three stones nestled in the fire. Even if Mama was right about the curse, Sukuma ancestors didn't really have rules about moving. Shida knew from the stories that had been passed down to her that Sukuma people had moved in the past. Those moves were still celebrated today. So why would the ancestors curse them for moving this time?

A figure suddenly blocked the golden light streaming in the door of the cooking hut.

"You're just putting a pot on now?"

Shida looked up to see Mama in the doorway. Her body looked as thin and burdened as a banana tree bent with heavy fruit.

"I had to go collect firewood," Shida said, "but it's alright, Mama. I've been thinking about this news of moving to Njia Panda, and it has to be good."

Mama slid down the front wall of the clay cooking hut into a crouch. She sighed. "Don't speak to me about this move, Shida. How can we leave Litongo? I've already lost so much — my husband, my honor as a woman in this village — and now I must lose my home?"

Shida leaned onto one arm, so that her head nearly touched the dirt floor. She blew at the fire and two new flames danced up from the glowing coals. A piece of wood popped, and the pot shifted on its rocks. Shida reached into the flames with her calloused hand and repositioned the pot. "Then tell me a story, Mama. Tell me the story about the Sukuma boy, Masala Kulangwa."

Usually, talk of stories calmed them both down, but this time Mama just closed her eyes. When she finally opened them, they reflected back a hazy stare in the glow of the firelight, like the village drunks' eyes when they went blurry from too much *pombe*.

Mama sighed. "Go out and pick some tomatoes so I can make a sauce for the corn porridge."

Shida stared at the ground. They had been in the fields today and both of them knew that their few sickly tomatoes were far from ripe. When Mama made a request like this for something they clearly did not have, she was really asking Shida to steal.

"It's nearly dark outside, Mama," Shida said. "Can't we just eat the *ugali* by itself?"

Mama sighed and closed her eyes. "Shida, just go! Go find something for us to wet this dry porridge with. Sitting here does no good."

Shida pushed herself up. "I'm going, Mama."

As Shida padded through the sandy yard, around the cattle corral, and past Babu's cooking hut, a woman's voice called out to her. "Sister Shida, where are you going?"

Shida peeked into the bright glow of the hut. One of her mother's sisters was sitting next to the fire. She usually came to cook for Babu in the evening, but only after she had cooked for her own children and husband.

"You're early, Aunty."

The woman sat tall on a stubby stool, and though her *kitenge* was just as worn as Mama's, she looked proud and beautiful in the firelight.

"My husband told me since I was already here for the meeting I could cook for Babu first tonight. But what are you doing?" She slapped Shida's knee playfully. "A young woman like you shouldn't be out alone at night. It's not right. People will talk."

Shida turned and looked into the yard. Even though Mama could be downright cruel, Shida didn't like complaining about her to anyone other than Grace or Babu.

"What's wrong, Shida? Is it your mother?"

Shida dragged her big toe in circles in the dirt. "She asked me to go out to our plot to pick some tomatoes for dinner."

"She — ! How can she send you out at this time of night? No wonder people say she's a witch." Her aunt turned to a pile of tomatoes and onions in the corner of the cooking hut. "Here. You see. I picked these for Babu, but there are too many for one old man to eat. Take some." She handed Shida two plump tomatoes and a smooth onion.

Aunty must have picked these tomatoes and onions not just for Babu, but for her own family as well. She was giving Shida some of her own dinner. Shida admired them in the firelight and then nodded. "Thank you, Aunty." She knew better than to reject a gift.

"You're looking more grown up these days, Shida." Her aunt slapped her on the leg again and smiled.

Shida looked up and winced to see her aunt staring at Shida's rapidly growing chest. For years, villagers had commented on Shida's muscular arms and legs or her enormous smile and perfect white teeth, but stares like these made Shida uncomfortable.

"I haven't gotten any taller," Shida said.

"No, not taller. Height isn't required for looking like a woman." Shida's aunt laughed. "Anyway, don't worry, Shida. Soon you'll be married and then your mother can't give you trouble. Marriage will suit you."

Shida pulled at her too-tight dress. She longed for the days when she still looked like a little girl, when there was no talk of marriage. Back then, Mama was kind to Shida when they were alone. She told Shida old Sukuma tales as they lay in their hut at night.

"Shida!" her aunt said. "You should go home, my child. You should be inside at this time of night."

Shida ran back to her own cooking hut. Mama was stirring their *ugali* to a thick consistency. Shida handed her the two tomatoes and, after hesitating for a moment, offered her the onion as well.

"Good, Shida. That was fast." Mama began peeling the onion with their dull kitchen knife.

Shida handed Mama their other pot and threw the

peeling scraps over her shoulder into the yard before propping herself up in the doorway. "Mama, I think this move to Njia Panda could be a good thing for us."

Mama grunted and raised her eyebrows.

"I could go to school and learn from the nurse. She could teach me how to become an even better healer and then when I'm older —"

"Shida, stop!" Mama put down the knife. Her eyes were suddenly focused. "You're a girl now, a child. Yes, you have healing skills. So did I when I was a girl. But how many medicine *women* do you know in our village?"

Shida stared at the flames. "But, Mama —"

"No, Shida. You don't know any. Only men. And now try to imagine one of these medicine women you dream about coming from what people call a dishonorable family, a family without a father. Do you see? That's you, Shida. Is that the sort of luck people are looking for when they go to a healer?"

"No," Shida said. She shifted back and forth between her feet and pulled at a hole in the waist of her dress.

"You have to understand this, Shida. Now, you're a girl. But tomorrow, you'll be a woman. People have room in their lives for girls with crazy mothers and dead fathers. They feel sorry for these girls. But when you grow up to become a woman, then honor becomes most important. How many fathers will choose to have their sons marry a young woman without a father? A young woman whose family has an unlucky history? Your best hope is to get married now while people still think of you as a girl."

Maybe Mama was right. Maybe Shida did need to get married soon, but the two married women Shida knew best were Mama and Aunty Grace, and marriage certainly hadn't done much for either of them. Mama's marriage had just brought her widowhood and shame, and Mama Grace was the unfavored wife of a grumpy man.

Mama straightened out her long torso from where she crouched in front of the fire. She leaned toward Shida. "You wanted me to tell you a story, Shida?"

Shida drew her head back. Was Mama serious? "Yes," she whispered.

"Alright, I'll tell you a story, Shida. Once, and this time, not so long ago, there was a young woman named Albina."

Shida glanced at Mama out of the corner of her eye. Albina had been Mama's name before she had Shida.

"Albina was beautiful and well known in her village of Litongo for her healing abilities. Albina carried a pouch on her waist full of herbs and tree bark and other medicines. Every boy in her village wanted to marry her, but her father wanted something better for Albina. He wanted her to be able to move to a new village that the trading men of Litongo said was on the shores of a great and beautiful lake. So her father selected a young man in this faraway village for her to marry. The young man's family sent her father ten cows for the dowry, and then her father walked with her for two long days through a forest, over hills, and across vast stretches of parched earth to her new home next to the lake.

"At first, she was happy. Her new husband, Milembe, was kind, and even though her mother-in-law made Albina work hard, Albina and Milembe had plans to build their own hut on their own land, where Albina could be in charge of everything. But Albina was already pregnant, and so Milembe promised that after the birth of their child, they would move.

"The months passed and Albina's belly and heart grew large with the hope of their new child and their family's future. But one day before the baby was born, Milembe suddenly grew very sick. Albina tried to heal him with her herbs, but her belly had already started to heave with the birth of the baby. Eventually she had to leave her husband to concentrate on herself. That night, Milembe died, and the next morning, Albina delivered a tiny baby girl. When Albina's mother-in-law set her eyes on the girl, she spat on the dry earth and named the girl 'Shida.' The mean old woman said Albina had upset the ancestors. She'd cursed Milembe and brought death to their family.

"Albina didn't know what to think. Maybe she had cursed Milembe. Maybe it'd been a mistake to leave her village. So she walked the long two-day journey back to Litongo all through that day and night, carrying the baby, Shida. When she arrived, she gave away her special medicine pouch and vowed never to leave her village again."

Mama sat staring at the flames. Her eyes were rimmed with tears.

"I'm sorry, Mama," Shida said. She reached out and put her hand on her mother's. "I know Father's mother was very mean to you. But who did you make that vow to, Mama? The ancestors? I don't think the ancestors will punish us for leaving Litongo. I think this move will be good. We'll get new fields and huts, and the nurse will help to heal us when we're sick, and I can go to their school."

Mama looked up. "Go to school, Shida?" Her eyes flashed back red firelight. "Here we are, not able to grow our own tomatoes because I have no other children to help us with our work, no husband to join us in the fields, and you talk of sitting with one of these teachers all day, while I work alone? *They* will not teach you how to be a proper young woman. What good will come of that?" Mama leaned back against the clay wall and unraveled her ratty head wrap. Wild tufts of matted hair stuck out above her sweaty face.

"Then I could help you farm and spend my free time learning from the nurse. If I learned all about her ways of healing, I could earn us money, Mama. With money, we could buy tomatoes and nice things like sugar and cooking oil. We could pay other villagers to help us grow cotton, and that would bring us more money. I could even buy you nice new *kitenge* cloth like Mama Kulwa's."

The fire popped. Mama's shoulders stiffened.

"Mama Kulwa! You would have your own mother look like Mama Kulwa?" Mama batted the empty pot next to her foot into the fire and heaved herself up to her feet. Shida stumbled backward out the door, but not fast enough to avoid a shove from Mama. Shida fell with a hard *smack* onto her bottom in the dirt yard.

"Why don't you just go sleep at Mama Kulwa's house tonight?" Mama hissed. "Don't come back until morning."

Shida gasped for air. Her bottom stung from the fall and her lungs ached for the air that had been knocked out of her, but the pain was more than that. Shida's eyes welled up with tears. How could Mama push her own child out of her home at night? Why couldn't Mama just treat her like a little girl again and tell her nice stories? But Mama's stiff posture in the doorway told Shida she needed to sleep elsewhere.

Shida got to her feet and shuffled the long way around the cattle corral to the path that led to Uncle Bujiko's compound where Mama Grace, Mama Kulwa, and Uncle Bujiko's third wife lived. She kept her eyes down, not wanting to see Babu or her aunt — she didn't need any more pity tonight. But as Shida began to jog up the path, she stopped, her eyes square with the dark form of a man's chest.

"Are you alright, child?" Babu's deep voice radiated through the warm night air.

Shida nodded and stared at the gentle shadow cast by Babu's walking stick in the moonlight.

"Where are you going at this time of night, my daughter?"

Shida shot a quick glance at Babu to see if he already knew the answer to this question, then averted her tear-brimmed eyes. Babu was like an old lion who had given up fighting and instead prowled around his territory ensuring that no one violated the peace. Of course, he had overheard everything.

"I'm going to Mama Grace's house to sleep," Shida said. "I said something about Mama Kulwa and Mama got angry and told me to go sleep there."

Shida didn't have to explain that she couldn't sleep at Mama Kulwa's house. Mama Kulwa would hardly let Shida step inside her hut, let alone spend a night with her. She was Uncle Bujiko's first wife, the most beautiful and the most spoiled, too. Like some of the men of Litongo, Uncle Bujiko had more than one wife, and like all of those men, he made it clear which wife was his favorite. Every New Year, Uncle Bujiko gave Mama Kulwa a brand-new pair of *kitenge* cloth squares printed with bright colors and patterns. His other two wives simply got her old ones. Uncle Bujiko favored Mama Kulwa not only because she was beautiful, but also because she had given him three boys, the first two being twins. The second wife was Mama Grace, who had given him two girls, Grace and Furaha. Girls were okay, because they brought their families cows for the bride price when they were married, but Uncle Bujiko was more interested in expanding his cotton farm, and he said he would need sons to direct that. His third wife was still quite young and had yet to give him any children.

"You're certain your mother won't have you back tonight?" Babu leaned on his walking stick and looked down at Shida.

"She won't have me," Shida said.

"Then it'll be good for you to spend a night with your cousin Grace," Babu said. "Can I send your aunty with you? She's just finishing with the cooking and she can accompany you on the walk."

Shida looked Babu square in the eye. "I'll be fine, thank you, Babu. I'd rather walk there on my own."

Babu nodded. He wouldn't consider allowing another girl Shida's age to walk alone at this time of night. There were venomous mamba snakes, and though the Serengeti lions in Babu's stories never came close to Litongo, smaller mountain lions sometimes ventured down from the hills. But Shida was special — she'd practically raised herself and once she had even killed a mamba snake with the dull blade of a *jembe* hoe.

Babu placed his right palm on her head. Her matted hair pushed down under the pressure of his calloused hand, and for a moment, Shida closed her eyes.

"Go as you like, my child. Just be safe."

"I will go carefully, Babu," Shida said. "Sleep in peace."

Shida raced through the darkness toward Grace's compound, zipping through familiar mounded rows of cassava and sweet potato plants. When she finally leaned in the doorway of Grace's hut, which was lit by the glow of a single kerosene light, Shida's heavy breathing was drowned out by a chorus of welcomes. Her two cousins and aunt were sitting like proper Sukuma women with their legs stretched out straight in front of them, leaning toward a tray of rice and beans. Saliva gushed into Shida's mouth.

"Welcome, Shida," Mama Grace said. "Come eat with us."

The two girls slid apart, making their triangle of legs into an open square with room for Shida to close it on the fourth side of the metal tray. Grace offered up a quick grin before turning back to the food, but once Shida had settled down beside her, Grace reached around and placed her hand on her cousin's feet. Of course she knew something bad had happened with Mama.

Furaha, who was six, jumped onto her knees and interlaced her rice-covered right hand with her left.

Shida flinched, but smiled. Left hands were for cleaning your bottom after going to the pit toilet, not for touching food.

"Oh, Shida!" The little girl almost sang as she tugged at the neckline of her faded pink blouse. "What is this village like that we'll move to? You must know something! You've talked to Babu, haven't you? Mama and Grace are so quiet. They won't answer any of my questions."

Shida laughed. The little girl's name — Furaha — was perfect. It meant "happiness" in Swahili, and Furaha was the happiest child Shida knew. In her first year of life, Furaha had been sick with diarrhea and almost died twice. That was probably why Mama Grace and Grace were so patient with her.

"Let your cousin eat first, my daughter. She must be hungry, and you know it's not polite to talk while eating." Mama Grace pointed at her own legs and raised her eyebrows.

Furaha sat back down and stretched out her legs. Her head jerked around the room distractedly. Shida smiled at the way her little cousin pinched up her tiny mouth, mustering every ounce of self-control she had to stay quiet.

Suddenly Furaha's round cheeks dropped. "Did your

Mama yell at you again, Shida?"

"Furaha!" Grace said.

"Are you okay, child?" Mama Grace studied Shida.

Shida nodded, feeling a lump rise in her throat. Her aunt's face was round and kind, so unlike Mama's. As always, Mama Grace kept her hair trimmed short and unbraided, unlike the other village women who spent hours each week changing their cornrow braids to other woven patterns.

"I'm fine," Shida said. "But may I sleep here tonight?"

"Of course," Mama Grace said.

For the rest of the meal, they ate in silence, kneading handfuls of rice into little cups and scooping up the beans. Afterward, they placed the empty tray in the yard to be washed the next morning, and Grace swept the bits of Furaha's dropped rice out the door. They pulled out their cowhide sleeping mats from under a bench on one wall. Tonight, rather than allowing the girls some space to whisper, Mama Grace angled the head of her mat toward the middle of the room. Shida hiccupped — maybe even Mama Grace would gossip about the move.

The two older girls hopped onto Grace's sleeping mat, still wearing their dresses, and pulled a tattered *kitenge* cloth taut over their close bodies to protect them from the mosquitoes that buzzed around them in the humid night air.

Mama Grace blew out the kerosene lamp and they all lay in complete darkness.

"Did Babu tell you anything more about Njia Panda tonight?" Grace said.

Shida propped herself up on one elbow, breaking the seal of the *kitenge* cloth on her side of the mat. "No, I was too busy fighting with Mama. She says we'll be cursed for leaving Litongo, but I don't think so. Do you, Grace? I think the ancestors will be happy to have us go to school."

"The ancestors might be happy," Grace said, "but my father came by our hut this evening and said that none of his daughters will ever go to school. He said maybe his boys will go if these teachers can teach good magic, like how to make cotton grow faster or how to build a motor car, but not his girls."

"But Babu will force him to let you go, Grace. Babu likes the nurse and he decided we'd move, so he'll probably want us to go to school. Anyway, what do you think it's like, this school? Will we each have our own huts for learning? Or will we sit in the teachers' compounds?"

"People say we'll learn to write words made out of those stick figures that look like people," Grace said.

Shida thought of the many times they had watched Uncle Bujiko trace numbers in the dirt when he negotiated with the cotton buyers from other villages.

"So we'll have to be outside in a dirt yard with sticks to

draw," Shida said.

Mama Grace rolled over on her mat. "*Shhh*. You should sleep, girls. The sun won't wait to rise with you in the morning."

And so they were quiet, but Shida couldn't sleep. What would life be like in Njia Panda?

Chapter 3

The horse that arrives early gets good drinking water.
— *South African proverb*

After the announcement of the move, Babu spent his days silencing rumors and making speeches about the importance of the move. Some people said the move was all a hoax invented by the people of Njia Panda, and Nyerere knew nothing of it: the people of Litongo would go over the hills only to be taken prisoner and forced to do farm work. Others said there would be no food in Njia Panda, that they would go over the hills and starve. Babu was patient. He understood his fellow villagers' fears and assured them that life would be good, even better on the other side of the hills. Nyerere would be proud of them and provide for them, and their children's children would tell stories about how, many years ago, the people of Litongo had had the courage to move — the courage to start a new Tanzania.

Eventually, the young men of Litongo left for Njia Panda to clear land for new plots and to build new huts. For the first month, most of the women and children stayed behind to wait for their rice harvest. Shida joined them, racing out to Mama's small rice field every morning to pray for rain and to build up the mud walls that served as catchments for their paddy. When the rice was finally ready for harvest, Shida drained their small parcel, cut the stalks to dry in the sun, and then beat them against the hard earth to separate the grain. In past years, Mama had complained that their paddy was too large for even two of them to tend, but this year, Shida did all the work alone.

Mama spent her days and nights lying in the cool darkness of their hut. Her only movement came twice a day when she propped herself up on one elbow to eat the food Shida brought her and then stumbled to the outhouse to relieve herself. For as long as Shida could remember, Mama had been angry and silent with the other villagers of Litongo, but she had always had energy for working and talking with Shida. Now, she didn't even scold Shida. Children whispered the word "witch" more and more when they passed by Mama's hut. Though Mama never mumbled to the ancestors or collected herbs to make bad medicines like real Sukuma witches did, Shida couldn't blame people for calling Mama names.

On the day when Shida had finally bagged up the last of their threshed rice, she ran into their hut and crouched on all fours, placing her head next to her mother's. Mama faced the back wall.

"Mama, it's done. We've got three full bags of rice. That's enough to keep us fed for months in Njia Panda. We can move now, Mama. It's perfect. Mama Grace and her children are leaving tomorrow. We can go with them. Babu says Uncle Bujiko has finished building our hut in the new village."

Mama rolled over on her mat.

Shida had to squint to read her mother's face in the darkness.

"How will we carry three bags of rice, Shida?"

Shida sat back on her knees. She hadn't thought of that. It hardly seemed important. "We'll find a way, Mama. But at least we can go now."

"What way, Shida? Will the little brothers and sisters you never had help us to carry our rice over the hills? What about your dead father? Will he be helping us?"

Shida gasped.

Mama's eyes seemed to pierce Shida's chest. "We'll leave for Njia Panda when there are two bags of rice left, only then."

"But it will take us at least one month to eat the first bag of rice, Mama. I can find someone to help us carry it."

Mama propped herself up to lean against the wall. Her hair stuck out in three angry tufts. "We don't need other people's help, Shida. We'll leave when there are two bags of rice."

Shida shuffled out of the hut, staring at her calloused hands and her muscular arms, which had grown even stronger after the last month's work. Why had she prayed for so much rain? Why had she worked so hard for their harvest? She slumped down in the dirt yard, too tired even to cry.

Over the course of the next month, Shida watched the rest of the villagers leave. With each family that walked off toward the hills, Shida lost each of her lingering doubts and fears about moving to Njia Panda. Instead, she felt as if she were sinking further into Litongo, further from her dreams of school and working with the nurse.

Then came the day that Babu left. One of the men who had moved right after the announcement appeared at their compound that morning. The elders had several important decisions to make in Njia Panda and they couldn't wait any longer for Babu. So Babu packed his few possessions and ducked into Mama's hut.

"Mama Shida, get up."

Shida watched from the doorway. Mama's body lay still.

"Mama Shida, I am your father. Get up."

Mama heaved herself up with two arms and sat in a slump, half facing Babu.

"I know you don't want to make this move. I know the idea of leaving Litongo only brings back the bad memories of the first time you left this village for your marriage, but that bad fortune is behind you and it's time to go. I've just sent my cattle ahead, including the cow, Milembe, that you dedicated to your husband. We should all follow."

Mama's head jerked up. Her eyes settled on Shida in the doorway.

Shida bent at the waist, pretending to snatch something up from the ground.

"Shida, go collect water from the river."

Shida ran to the edge of the compound to grab their pail. But the pail and their clay water barrel were already full — she'd filled them that morning.

When Babu emerged from Mama's hut, his face was lined with worry. He hobbled over to Shida, where she squatted at the base of the mango tree. "She's promised me to leave in two days, when there are only two bags of rice left."

Shida stared up at Babu. How could Mama possibly know? She hadn't touched a cooking pot or their bags of rice in nearly a month, but she was right — there was exactly enough grain to last them two more days before they finished the first sack of rice.

⚹⚹⚹⚹⚹⚹⚹⚹⚹⚹⚹⚹⚹⚹

Two days later, Shida got up before the sun rose, tied on her medicine pouch, and ran down the path to the last compound, other than her own and those of the four families who had chosen to stay behind, that was still inhabited. Shida could just see Mama Lewanga squatting outside her empty hut in the light of dawn. Her toddler, Baby Lewanga, rested in her lap.

"Oh, Shida," Mama Lewanga said, "you've really worked magic. He's fine now, just a little tired. For a while, I thought he'd leave us like the other two, but now he's better."

Shida smiled and walked over to the woman. She remembered the fear in Mama Lewanga's eyes three days ago when she'd called Shida to heal Baby Lewanga. The little boy's body had been raging with heat. Many children in Litongo died from fever or bad diarrhea, but Mama Lewanga had already lost two children in the years before Shida started healing.

"Have you finished the tea?" Shida asked the little boy. She'd made a strong brew of bark from the *mamihigo* tree, and visited three times a day to make sure he drank the medicinal tea.

Baby Lewanga's eyes were closed as he rested in his mother's lap, but the minute Shida said the word "tea," he twisted up his face.

"He says he doesn't need to finish it, Shida. I tried to make him drink the little bit left in our cooking pot, but he kept asking for you."

Shida sat down in the dirt next to Mama Lewanga and pulled the toddler into her lap. "Hello, Baraka," she cooed. Shida called all of her patients Baraka, which meant "blessing" in Swahili.

Baby Lewanga opened his eyes and smiled up at her.

"I hear you're going to Njia Panda today, Baraka," Shida said.

The boy blinked back at her.

"You're such a lucky boy. Your father and all of your friends are waiting for you there. People say the roofs of the houses in Njia Panda are made of metal, like the blades of our *jembe* hoes. I even heard they're saving the shiniest roof in the whole village just for you."

The little boy glanced up at the thatch roof just above them.

"But in order to make the very long, long journey to Njia Panda, Baraka, you must drink this special tea. It'll make you strong and fast, as fast as the big cats who run across the Serengeti plains. Don't you want to be strong and fast, Baraka?"

The boy eyed his mother and then Shida. He pushed himself up in Shida's lap and reached for the pot with his plump hands.

Shida placed the pot's rim on his tiny lips and Baby Lewanga tipped it back, guzzling all of the tea without taking a single breath.

After Shida said goodbye to Mama Lewanga and the little boy, she ran back up the road toward Mama's hut and ducked through the door. Mama was there on the floor, her back to the door.

"Mama!" Shida winced at the forcefulness of her own voice. "Mama, we promised Babu we'd leave today. We promised. Even Mama Lewanga and her child have gone — they said they hoped to see us on the trail."

Mama groaned and rolled over on her reed mat to face Shida. Her eyes were closed, but she parted her dry lips. "There's at least a half cup of rice left, Shida."

Shida sighed. "Yes, it's left over from last night. Here." She dashed out of the hut and returned with their smallest pot lined with a thin layer of cooked rice and a second pot sloshing with a weak brew of tea. "Eat. I'll prepare our things."

Shida's stomach growled as she snatched up her second dress, their two reed sleeping mats, two hoes, one bucket, their third metal pot, and two wooden cooking spoons. In the yard, she tied everything into the first square of Mama's spare pair of *kitenge* cloth and nodded to herself — she'd carry this bundle. In the second square she would tie their two remaining cooking pots for Mama to carry. Each of them would take a sack of rice.

"We're ready, Mama. Let's go." Shida stared at the darkened doorway.

A breeze rustled the leaves of the mango tree.

Shida gritted her teeth. What was wrong with Mama? Part of Shida just wanted to leave her behind.

"If I tell you a story, will you come, Mama?"

Darkness stared back at Shida. She took a deep breath and settled down in the dirt yard.

"Alright, Mama. Listen to me. This is our favorite story. This is the story of Masala Kulangwa and the Shing'weng'we monster." Shida's chest was still tight with frustration, but she tried to relax. "This is the story you used to tell me when I was sad, Mama. This story made me happy."

And so Shida retold Mama the story of the boy Masala Kulangwa, whose village had been attacked by a monster. All the villagers had been eaten, except Masala's mother, who was pregnant and who had managed to hide. As the boy grew up and understood what had happened to his people, he grew determined to go out and kill the monster, the Shing'weng'we. But since he did not know what the monster looked like, each day he came home with a new animal he had killed — first a grasshopper, then a bird, a gazelle, and finally an antelope.

"Do you remember what Masala Kulangwa said each

time he returned with a new dead animal, Mama?" Shida batted at a fly buzzing around her head.

"I'll tell you, Mama. Each time Masala Kulangwa said, 'Mother, Mother, I've killed Shing'weng'we up in the hills. Rejoice and shout for joy.'

"But his mother always answered: 'My dear one, this is only an antelope, not the monster. The monster still roams.'

"Finally, Masala Kulangwa found the Shing'weng'we monster. They fought long and hard, but the clever boy won by splitting the monster's stomach open. Out came his father and all the other villagers. But in the process of cutting the monster open, Masala Kulangwa had sliced off an old lady's ear. She was angry and threatened to bewitch him, but Masala Kulangwa gathered some herbs, pounded them into a poultice, and applied them to her wound. Her ear grew back. All of the villagers were happy, so they raised him up on a three-legged stool designed for a chief!

"And from that day forward, Mama, Masala Kulangwa became chief of the world, and his mother was the Queen Mother.

"The end."

The yard hummed with an eerie silence — there were no cattle mooing, no dogs barking in the distance, no neighbors' roosters crowing.

"Mama, we don't want to be like Masala Kulangwa and his mother — we don't want to be the only ones left behind."

Mama ducked through the hut's doorway and into the golden, sun-drenched morning. Shida stumbled back to get out of her way, feeling a weight in her stomach. No wonder Mama shaded her eyes with one hand and gripped her waist with the other. Lying around in the dark for the last two months hadn't been good for her — the muscles in her arms and shoulders had withered away, and her cheek was lined with the indents of her reed mat.

A lump rose in Shida's throat. So, this was it. She had been so busy trying to goad Mama into moving that she had never thought about how it would feel to leave. The mango tree glowed in the morning light. Shida would never pick one of its fruits again. The worn wooden doorframe of her hut suddenly looked lonely. Shida would never pass through it again. She turned and looked out at the cluster of trees that lined the Litongo river. Never again would she feel the cool relief of stepping into those waters to fill a bucket. And — Shida bit her lip as she stared at Mama's hunched back — she might never again have a mother who was healthy or kind, even just to her.

"Let's go," Mama said.

Shida blinked back her tears. "Yes, Mama. Let's go."

They reached the top of the hills well past noon. Shida squatted down and let her bundle and sack of rice slide to the ground with a great *clang* and *thump*. She ran her hand across her sweaty brow, but then her eyes settled on the valley below. "Mama!"

Mama shuffled up behind Shida, wheezing.

"Mama, look at the village! Look at all the shiny, metal rooftops. And . . ." Shida's eyes darted back and forth across the wide expanse of Njia Panda. Fields radiated outward in rings around a tight cluster of huts lined with wide roads.

"What could those be?" Shida hiccupped and pointed to three enormous gray boxes at the middle of the village — each of them looked big enough to house five huts.

The vulture that had followed them up the hill screamed from the hot air above. Shida shook out her arms and legs. She was ready to run for hours down the hill and across the fields until they reached Njia Panda, but when Shida turned to Mama, she froze.

Mama's arms were trembling and her face was stiff and gray as she stared down at their new home.

"Mama, we're going to be fine. Look at this beautiful village. Life has to be good there."

One of Mama's eyelids twitched.

"Here, Mama, give me your rice sack," Shida said. She loaded her own sack of rice and bundle onto her head and then squatted down next to Mama, dragging the second sack of rice onto her shoulder. Shida's knees nearly buckled under the weight, but she forced herself to stand, and then took two steps forward.

For the next three hours, they stumbled down the treacherous path. Even though Shida kept pace with Mama, in her mind she was running ahead, running to Grace and Babu and their new home in Njia Panda.

When the path flattened out, they zigzagged through small, untilled plots and later through much larger fields lined with spindly maize stocks, green sweet potato leaves, young tomato vines, and spinach seedlings.

At the edge of the last field, someone sat outside a ring of three huts with shiny metal roofs. Shida ran to see who it was, but when she recognized the broad shoulders of her Uncle Bujiko, she slowed to a walk.

"*Ny'wadela*, Uncle Bujiko." Shida greeted her uncle in their tribal language. So one of these huts was Grace's home.

"Address me properly, girl."

Shida's brow furrowed. She had greeted him with the most respectful words possible. Did he really expect her to bend down on one knee? Shida began to crouch, but stumbled. She'd have to drop her bags.

"Don't." Mama's hoarse voice cut through the warm evening air.

Shida froze.

"Don't drop the rice, Shida. How will you pick it up again? Besides, you don't need to bow down to him."

Shida glanced up at her uncle.

"So, this is the thanks you give me for building you a new hut and clearing a field for you, Sister?" Uncle Bujiko said.

"Do I owe you thanks, Brother?" Mama said. "I see you have chosen the compound nearest the fields to lessen your walk to your farm. And it looks as if you've chosen the biggest and closest field as your own. Something tells me *my* walk from *my* hut to *my* small plot will be much longer."

The corner of Shida's mouth turned up in a smile. At least Mama was getting back her energy for arguing with Uncle Bujiko. The two of them never seemed to get along. Babu said their feuding dated back to when they were children. Mama had had a talent for healing at a young age and enjoyed full run of the village. Uncle Bujiko had been sick throughout his early childhood with fever. Villagers had labeled him as weak, and instead of going out on trading expeditions with the men or pasturing the cows with other young boys, he had been made to stay home and rest with the old women. Maybe that was why he was always trying to prove himself as a man.

"Oh, you crazy woman. You've no idea how much I've worked to build this new village. And the sacrifices! I've left behind over half my cattle on loan to the old *mganga's* son in Litongo. There's no grazing land here. All of my cotton fields have been abandoned, but at least I'm not the one who brought a curse on herself for leaving Litongo. You know the ancestors will curse you again for leaving."

Uncle Bujiko pivoted on his stool to face the two smaller huts on his compound — the third was much larger and rectangular, unlike any Shida had seen before. That one had to be Mama Kulwa's.

"Furaha!" Uncle Bujiko shouted.

Led by her little round belly, Furaha skipped out of one of the smaller huts' shadowy doorways.

"Shida!" The little girl squealed. Furaha ran toward her cousin, but when her eyes settled on Mama, she stumbled to a stop.

"Take your ungrateful aunt and cousin to their new home," Uncle Bujiko said.

Furaha shuffled forward a few steps, gripping the skirt of her striped dress.

"Go, child!"

Furaha walked a big circle around Mama, then scurried up the road with Shida hurrying behind her. Shida stared, dumbstruck, at the houses that came one after another in dense clusters.

"Welcome, Shida! Welcome to your new home." Voices sang out from every corner of the road.

"It's beautiful, Furaha," Shida said. Her eyes flitted over metal roofs, huts with mud walls freshly sealed with cow dung, and compounds already planted with flowers. At the side of the road, a woman lifted a metal lever up and down. Shida watched water splash into an empty bucket. She stopped and hiccupped. As long as the woman lifted and lowered the metal stick, water flowed into her pail.

"Who made this, Furaha? Was it the young medicine man?"

Furaha giggled. "Gracey calls it a pump, and she says the government gave it to us for living here, but I think it must be some sort of magic."

After a few more curves in the road, Furaha stopped in front of a small compound. "Cousin Shida." Furaha tipped her tiny head toward the cattle corral in the yard.

One of the cows in the crowded corral mooed loudly and stuck its head over the brambles, staring at Shida. The cow's head was black and lined with a white stripe that started at its nose.

"Milembe?" Shida grinned. It was Mama and Shida's only cow — the one they had dedicated to Shida's dead father by giving it his name. Behind the corral were two new clay huts with shimmering metal roofs and a small cooking hut.

Shida laughed out loud and leaned forward to let the two sacks of rice and the big bundle fall from her shoulders

and roll into the side of the corral. "This is it. We're home."
She leapt into the air. "Babu? Where's Babu? We're home."

Shida raced around the yard. There was a small mango tree, just like in Litongo. And . . . her eyes scanned up a round, gray wall. There, behind their two huts, was an enormous kopje, a granite outcropping that looked like a giant's oval building block balanced on end. Shida wiped her sweaty hands on her dress and ran toward the rock. She lunged to grab a notch halfway up the face.

"Don't." Mama's raspy voice yanked Shida back to the ground. "Young women don't climb rocks and trees."

Shida gritted her teeth. The view from the top of that rock had to be amazing. She'd be able to see all of Njia Panda. But Shida knew better than to defy her mother.

"Welcome, my daughters." Babu's deep, measured voice radiated from the corner of the dirt yard as he stepped out of one of the huts.

Shida turned and dipped down on one bended knee. There he was, Babu. Everything about him made Shida feel at home — his knotted walking stick, his stained white shirt, and his bony face glowing in the light of the setting sun.

"I'm glad you've come today," he said. "School starts tomorrow, and this way you can begin with the others, Shida."

"School?" Mama's voice was shrill. "But, Father, who'll

help me with all of the chores? I don't have a husband, no other children. How will we farm with only *my* hands? How will we eat?"

"You'll work on the new village farm, my daughter," Babu said. "The village will provide food for you. And in the afternoons, I'll send Bujiko's girl, Grace, to help Shida do her chores. But my grandchildren will go to school, all of them. Our children have learned many things in Litongo, but this school will teach them about other medicines, and about how to make their vegetable crops healthy, about the books we've seen merchant men from other villages use, and maybe even about the magic used to power the trucks that brought the metal for our houses to this village. It's important that all of our children go to school."

Shida hiccupped. So Grace and Furaha would go to school, too.

"This place is a curse, Father," Mama said. "Remember how you told me before I left Litongo for my marriage that going away would help me? You said my husband's village would have more people for me to heal and more food to eat. You said it would be better there. But it wasn't. And now you think this school and this new village will be better for Shida? They won't be. You'll see. We should never have left Litongo." Mama disappeared into their new hut.

Shida stared up at the little mango tree behind their new home and at the beautiful kopje. How could Mama be so negative?

"We'll be fine here, Babu. I'll work hard and I'll try to help Mama."

"I know you will, my child."

But when Shida turned to look at Babu, his eyes were lined with worry.

Chapter 4

Knowledge is better than riches.
— *Cameroonian proverb*

Shida bounced with each step down the road to school. "Come on!" she shouted back at Grace and Furaha. She was wearing the nicer of her two dresses. It was dark green and had once been decorated with a pattern of black dotted lines, zigzagging around like the path of a bumblebee. Like her yellow dress, it was three years old, but at least it wasn't quite so tight around the hips and chest.

Grace walked with a measured pace, scanning everything on their path as if she were trying to memorize it all. Furaha leapt along the sandy road, struggling to keep up.

They reached a rise in the road and looked down on three enormous, gray, boxy buildings with slanted metal roofs. These were what Shida had seen when she and Mama crested the hills on their way from Litongo.

"They're huge!" Shida said. "What are they?"

"One's the school, one's the nurse's clinic, and one's for village meetings," Grace said. "How do you think they got such enormous sheets of metal to cover them?"

But Shida was off, careening down the hill toward the school, where a pack of children had already gathered in the shade of a flamboyant tree speckled with red blossoms.

Shida squatted next to a group of boys in the schoolyard as she caught her breath. Her eyes jumped from the smooth gray walls of the schoolhouse to the perfect miniature cacti and bougainvillea cuttings.

"Oh, how wonderful to see a young girl here. Welcome to the new Njia Panda School!"

Shida turned to the gentle voice that had greeted her, but her eyes met a belt buckle. She craned her head up and farther up along a man's tall, skinny body until she saw an angular face smiling down at her.

"I'm very pleased to see you here. I hope you bring other girls." The man patted Shida on the shoulder, but as he withdrew his hand, Shida flinched. Where his three middle fingers should have been were three stumps.

The man moved on through the crowd, towering over children and parents.

"What are you doing here?" A voice boomed behind

Shida.

She turned to face a short, stocky man.

He leaned toward her with a mouthful of stained teeth. "Answer me! Why are you here?"

Shida stared. Why was he so angry?

"We're here for school." Grace walked around the man and stood next to Shida.

Shida grabbed her cousin's hand.

"This is very serious," he roared. "Girls don't belong at this school, or any school, for that matter. Do your parents know you're here?"

"Our grandfather sent us." Grace's voice was as cool as the water that had flowed out of the pump that morning.

The short, fat man glared at the giant teacher, who was now talking with a group of boys at the other end of the schoolyard. "This is crazy. Everyone knows girls should be at home learning to cook and clean. Teacher Mrefu isn't the only teacher here. I'll make it easy for you to decide you never want to come back."

Shida, Grace, and Furaha stood silently at the edge of the crowd, eyeing the stout man as he stormed off through the growing crowd. There were boys everywhere — in fact a group of them was forming around Shida and her cousins — but only a few girls.

Finally, the tall teacher waved both his arms in the air to get everyone's attention.

"Look at his ugly hand," a boy near Shida said.

"What could've done that?" another muttered. "A witch?"

"Welcome to Njia Panda School," the tall man said. "My name is Teacher Mrefu, and I'm your head teacher."

The students laughed.

Teacher Mrefu smiled. "I'm glad to see that even here in Sukumaland your knowledge of the Swahili language is good. Yes, *mrefu* does mean tall, but that is indeed my name." He turned and pointed to the stocky teacher. "This is Teacher Karakola."

Teacher Karakola glared back at the crowd.

"All of you will be split into two groups, one for older students and one for younger students." Teacher Mrefu pointed to a scar on the flamboyant tree's trunk. "We'll have each of you stand against this tree. Those who are above the mark will be my students. We'll stay in the schoolyard today. And those who are below the mark will go to the schoolroom with Teacher Karakola. We'll take turns using the classroom, but your classmates and teacher will remain the same for the year."

I'm a big girl, right?" Furaha whispered. "I'll make it into the big class, right, Shida?"

Shida gripped Furaha's hand as Grace walked up to the tree. Grace rolled her shoulders up and back to meet the trunk and stared straight ahead. She kept her feet flat on the ground, but she stretched her neck and spine, looking even taller than she normally did.

"The young class!" Teacher Karakola said.

"No," said Teacher Mrefu. He nudged Grace forward with his stumpy hand. "She looks like she's just over the mark, and besides, my older students will benefit from having some girls in the class."

Grace's chest relaxed and Shida stifled a hiccup.

Furaha charged up to the tree. "I'm a big girl," she said to Teacher Mrefu. "I should be in the big class."

Teacher Mrefu laughed. Furaha was at least three hands' distance from the mark. "You're a very big girl," he said. "But, lucky you, you aren't too big, which means that you get to go in the young class now and then in a couple of years, you'll get to go in the older class. That way when you leave school, you'll have learned twice as much."

Furaha's shoulders dropped and her lips turned down in a pout, but she ran off toward three of their female cousins who had been assigned to the younger class.

Shida was next. There was no chance Teacher Mrefu would take her — she'd always been short for her age. Shida glanced up at the scar as she turned her back to the tree.

But Teacher Mrefu waved her to the side anyway. "We need one more girl for the older class. Stand over there."

When the class assignments had been made, Teacher Mrefu gathered his students at the base of the flamboyant tree. "Inside the classroom, you'll see that we have desks and chairs for students to share, but on days like today when we're outside, you'll have to make do sitting in the dirt yard."

Shida smiled at Grace. Having a desk and chair would be a dream, even if she had to share.

"Now, I'll expect you to sit in your assigned order," Teacher Mrefu said, "Just as if the desks and chairs were in the yard." He picked up a stick and made a grid of squares in the dirt, and then he turned to Grace and Shida. "Our two courageous female students. Where would you like to sit?" Grace and Shida picked a square at the front and then Teacher Mrefu continued with the assignments, only he didn't offer the boys a choice.

After they had all settled into their squares, Teacher Mrefu grabbed a big black board and a bundle of twigs from behind the tree. He leaned the board against the tree's trunk and then held out a bundle of twigs to Shida. "Please give one of these to each student."

Shida reached out to take the twigs, careful not to touch the teacher's stumpy hand, but as she began to pass out sticks, she felt her face grow warm. What was she afraid of? Teacher Mrefu was a nice man. So what if he was missing a few fingers?

"Not that one!" A boy seated directly behind Shida and Grace's box waved his hand at the stick Shida held out to him. His face was round as a full moon and his body nearly filled the square he was supposed to share with his desk mate. Normally, Shida found fat people handsome — all Sukuma did. Being fat meant you were rich and had plenty of food to eat. But there was something ugly about this boy's face.

"Give me that one," he said.

Shida handed him the longest stick in the pile. Who cared about stick length?

The boy smiled, narrowing his eyes. "You'll regret giving me this long stick."

"Quiet, Gervas," said Teacher Mrefu. "Scolding you this morning before class assignments were given was enough. I expect you to behave well for the rest of the day."

For the next couple of hours, Teacher Mrefu reminded the class how to count in Swahili from one to one hundred. For Grace and Shida, who had learned Swahili from Babu, this was easy, but some of the other students, who only knew Sukuma, struggled to keep up. After the students were comfortable counting, Teacher Mrefu pulled out a small white stick and traced a beautiful, clean, white line on the surface of the black board.

"This is the number one, *moja* in Swahili."

Shida hiccupped.

"This is . . ." Teacher Mrefu frowned at the second number he had written on the board and rubbed the curvy lines with the side of his fist. They disappeared and only a few particles of white dust remained on the board.

Shida gasped. She shot her hand up in the air just as Teacher Mrefu had taught them to do when they had a question. What magic had he used to make the white lines disappear? But at the same moment, the back of her arm seared with pain. Shida grabbed her throbbing tricep — an inflamed red line glared up from her healthy brown skin.

Another blow hit her back and Shida whipped around. Gervas. His round face bulged with a grin.

"Say something, and I'll hit you even harder after school with this nice stick you gave me," Gervas whispered.

When Shida and Grace were excused for the day, they stood on the road outside the school, waiting for Furaha. Shida scanned the village center, keeping a lookout for Gervas. Her eyes settled on the nurse's clinic, just two buildings away. "Grace, we could visit the nurse quickly, just to say hi."

Grace held up her hand. "Listen," she said.

Inside the schoolroom, a man's voice roared. "Your parents can't possibly want you here. School isn't for girls. Girls should learn to do chores and farm, not read. Reading is for boys and men."

The yelling continued for several minutes. Finally, students poured out of the classroom. A group of little boys scurried across the schoolyard, absolutely silent until they reached the road.

"School is for boys," one said, trying to copy Teacher Karakola's deep voice. "Reading's for boys, not girls." The others sniggered.

"What are you talking about?" Shida swung at the crowd of little boys and smiled as they scattered, but then she spotted Furaha.

The little girl was running out of the schoolroom with five female cousins. Tears were running down her chunky cheeks. Grace squatted in the yard, holding out her hands, and Furaha dove into them.

"He told us not to come back tomorrow. The teacher said school isn't for girls, only for boys. It's not true, is it, Grace? The teacher isn't right."

Shida gathered the other young girls into her arms, but she kept her eyes on Grace and Furaha.

"You'll be okay," Grace said.

Furaha put her small hands on Grace's shoulders and shoved her sister back. She stamped. "Say it, Grace. Say he isn't right. He can't tell us not to come to school."

"You'll be okay," Grace repeated. Shida noticed that her cousin didn't actually say whether girls should be there or not. Grace just stared at the schoolhouse over Furaha's shoulder.

Chapter 5

Rain beats a leopard's skin, but it does not wash out the spots.
— Ghanaian proverb

"Where have you been?" Shida sat in a cowhide chair, squinting through the darkness at Grace as she approached Babu's hut. "I thought you were going to help me with my chores. Mama didn't do a thing all day. I had to haul ten buckets of water from the pump, wash her *kitenge* and my yellow dress, scrub last night's cooking pots, and then cook dinner. I'm exhausted."

"Father wouldn't let me go," Grace said. She slumped into Babu's second cowhide chair. Shida could just make out the tired contours of Grace's face in the lantern light. "He said I had to cook dinner tonight and then he sat outside the cooking hut and went on and on about what a waste it is to put girls in school."

"But Babu told him you had to help *me* in the afternoons. How am I supposed to go to school and then come home and do all of this work?"

Babu shuffled out of his hut and into the darkness, humming. Shida jumped out of his chair and squatted next to it.

"Ah, thank you, Shida." Babu gripped the arms of the chair and lowered himself most of the way until he fell with a *thump*.

An owl hooted from across the road near the fan palm tree, and the three of them froze. Babu stopped humming.

All Sukuma knew owls were evil spirits and the friends of witches. If an owl appeared at your house, bad fortune was sure to come, and sometimes even death. People in Litongo had cut down trees near their houses to keep owls away, but Babu had refused to cut down their mango tree. Babu said the mangoes and the shade were gifts from his brother, the tree, and he couldn't possibly cut down a brother.

The palm fronds rustled, and then the black shadow of the owl flapped across the moon in the direction of the water pump and Uncle Bujiko's compound.

Babu exhaled. "Well, let's hope the owl won't bring us bad fortune. I'm sure it won't. Both of you are well, no?"

Grace kept her eyes down, but Shida sighed. "Actually,

Babu, not everything went well at school today. Our teacher seems very nice. He said he was happy to have us there, but the only girls who showed up were our cousins and there's this boy in our class who kept hitting us with sticks. The bigger problem, though, is the younger students' teacher . . ."

Babu's eyes widened and twitched with each new detail as Shida recounted the events of their day.

When Shida finished talking, Grace looked up. "Babu, please don't take us out of school."

Babu's forehead furrowed and his eyes locked with Grace's. "No, my daughter. No, you shouldn't worry about me taking you out of school. You girls will only stop school when you're ready, and I can't imagine that."

"Thank you, Babu," Shida said.

Babu turned to Shida and nodded. He was wearing his tattered white T-shirt, which was yellow around the neck and arms. But Shida still thought he looked regal in the moonlight. Regal in a soft way.

"Tomorrow's Saturday, so I'll speak with your teachers this weekend, but you must remain strong, strong like our first Sukuma ancestor, who named our tribe."

Shida smiled up at Grace. No matter what they talked about, Babu always managed to make a connection to their ancestors.

"Tell us the story about this ancestor, Babu," Grace said.

"*Ehh*, tell us, Babu," Shida said.

Babu folded his hands in his lap and squinted up toward the moon. He swayed in his chair, as if he had to feel the story before he could tell it. "A very long time ago, our people settled around our great lake here in Tanzania. They brought their cattle and they slowly grew, bearing children, who later bore children of their own. This growth was good, but you know how we Sukuma like our space?"

The girls nodded. They knew all too well. In public, Shida's people were holding their heads high, proud to be a part of one of Nyerere's first new villages, but Shida had already heard people muttering under their breaths about the lack of space and privacy in Njia Panda.

"Well, even then, even before we called ourselves 'Sukuma,' we liked our space. And so, as our people multiplied, our chief watched, pleased and yet worried at the same time, until eventually he decided something must be done. He called on his most beloved son and explained the problem to him.

"'My son,' he said. 'It's now time for our people to spread out, so that we can continue to multiply, but also be happy with enough space.'

"The chief told his son to take 250 men and women and walk until they found a place where there was plenty of space for all of them to settle. The son was frightened. He felt too young to be a chief, away from his family and in a new place. But he knew his father was right."

"And so what happened?" Shida asked.

"The young man took the men and women with him. They walked for many days, not satisfied with the dry land that they crossed. The chief's son worried he was leading them poorly, but one day they arrived at a huge cove in a lake. Everywhere, they saw enormous kopjes, just like the one behind our compound, Shida." Babu pointed to the lookout rock behind their huts. "But there in that cove, there was a pile of oddly-shaped kopjes that jutted up through the sparkling water like a pyramid.

"The people stared at the beautiful rocks and the green land that surrounded the lake's banks, and the young chief knew he had found a new home for his people. He turned to his people and announced, '*Nye-nsukumale-aha.*' 'Let us camp here.'

"The people knew he spoke wisely — he had taken on a frightening challenge and persevered until he found his people a home. And so for years, the young chief's people repeated his words, '*Nye-nsukumale-aha,*' until the words stuck and other tribes simply called us the Sukuma. That is how our tribe earned its name."

Babu rocked in his chair, and Shida watched the moonlight and shadows dance on his face. He was right. Like the young chief, Nyerere and Babu and all of the elders of Litongo were taking on a great challenge with this new village, asking their people to move, this time for less space in order to fulfill a dream. Everyone — including Shida, Grace, and Furaha as they began school — would have to have courage like the young chief's people did when they ventured out into new lands.

"We'll do it, Babu," Shida said. We'll work hard at school, and we'll help Furaha and the little ones deal with their mean teacher."

"Good, my daughter," Babu said. "I know you'll work hard. And in the end, I believe President Nyerere is leading us in a good direction. I believe we will find our rock pyramid in the middle of a sparkling lake."

Shida's eyes welled with tears. She turned to Grace. Grace was leaning back in her chair, gazing up at the stars. Her eyes sparkled in the moonlight and her cheeks, which had been taut with tension earlier that day, were round with hope.

"Before you go . . ." Babu thrust his walking stick into the dirt and heaved his old body up into a wobbly stance, "I have something for the two of you." He shuffled into his hut and emerged with two flat, rectangular objects in his hand. He handed one to each of the girls, along with two very straight twigs.

Shida looked more closely. The rectangle was an oversized book. Shida had never touched a book before. The inside of this book was blank; clean white pages shone up at her in the moonlight. She looked over at Grace's. Grace was gripping her twig and running one end of it along the delicate paper. It left a mark.

Shida drew her twig along a page in her book and then jumped up. "It's like the white stick Teacher used on his black board today!"

Babu smiled. "*Ehh*, these are your own books and tools for writing. And . . . turn the page of your book, Shida."

Shida turned it and watched a thin square of newsprint flutter to the ground. She picked it up and saw a picture of the nurse and Njia Panda's two teachers standing outside their school. Her eyes widened. Shida had never seen a picture of someone she knew before.

"But this is . . ." Shida stammered in her excitement.

Babu laughed. "Yes, our teachers and nurse. In the capital, they are writing stories about our new village. They say that this is a test village for the country. If we can manage to care for one another in Njia Panda, then more will follow our example and move to *ujamaa* villages in other parts of the country."

Shida stood up tall, rolling back her shoulders. Rather than feeling burdened, she was inspired knowing that others were watching them. Of course the move would be difficult. Of course villagers would grumble about girls going to school or about the long walk to the fields. They were taking on a new challenge. Shida and her people were charting new territory.

"Take good care of these books and record everything you learn," Babu said. "You two girls are like the young Sukuma chief who named our people. One day when you're old, like me, children will ask for your stories. They'll say, 'Grandmother, tell us about the time when you and Aunty were the first girls to go to school. What did you learn?' And if your memory is running away like mine, you'll look in your books and you'll remember."

Shida squeezed her book to her chest and hiccupped. "We'll do it, Babu. We'll record everything."

Grace nodded. "But I doubt that we'll ever forget."

Chapter 6

When the drumbeat changes, the dance changes.
— *Nigerian proverb*

Shida felt the coolness of her reed mat under her body, but she kept her eyes closed, trying to return to her dream. Endless stretches of water and immense granite kopjes. Something so peaceful. Where was this dream place?

But the din of men shouting and cows mooing outside her hut pulled Shida back to consciousness. She cracked her eyes open and lifted her head. Mama was standing in the doorway, outlined by the silvery light of dawn.

"They're gone. The cattle have been let loose." Mama's voice was as calm as the morning breeze that played with her *kitenge* skirt.

Shida sat up on her reed mat and stared at Mama. Her

teeth clenched. What did she mean, *gone?*

"Did Maasai warriors sneak in and raid the cattle?" Shida asked. She scrambled to her feet, but when she squeezed into the doorway next to Mama, she froze.

Out on the road, cows and people ran every which way. The thorny brambles that closed the circle of Babu's cattle corral were torn away. Babu's cows milled around the compound and the road, mixed in with neighbors' cattle.

"Who did this?" Shida said.

Mama turned from the doorway and flopped down on her reed mat. "We'll get the cows back, Shida." Mama almost sounded happy. "No one's saying anything about missing cows. They're just loose. I told you this place was cursed."

Shida's arms grew tense. A village full of cattle running loose was not about bad luck. *Someone* had done this. She could feel Mama's eyes boring into her back. Mama wanted to argue, but Shida stepped out of the doorway and rounded their hut. She stood in front of the kopje that loomed behind their hut. If ever there was a good time to climb up the enormous rock outcropping for a view of the village, it was now. Shida wedged her feet and hands into little nooks in the rock face and slowly pulled herself up. She crawled out to the front of the kopje.

When she looked up, Shida felt like a hawk, soaring over the village. The view spanned from the hills on one side to the horizon on the other. Off to the left, large stretches of fields were spotted with seedlings. Inside the ring of fields, rooftops glinted back the light of dawn. All along the road from Uncle Bujiko's compound, up to Babu's and out toward the big, gray box that was the school, hundreds of cows were loose, chomping on sprigs of grass, flowers, discarded corn husks, anything green they could find. Every man and boy from Litongo was running in circles, trying to direct the ambling beasts back home.

Shida's eyes jerked to her right, out beyond the school and clinic to the old section of the village that people were now calling Old Njia Panda. It was completely calm. Smoke rose from a single cooking hut.

Shida's face grew warm. Someone from Old Njia Panda must have done this, someone who didn't want Shida's people invading their village.

Shida squinted through the hot morning sun for the next two hours, looking for signs of anything unusual. Whoever had done this still had to be around, sneaking through New Njia Panda, enjoying the chaos. But all Shida saw were villagers from Litongo rounding up their own cows. When all of the corrals were closed up again, Shida flopped back on her giant lookout kopje.

Angry voices drifted up from the yard. Shida crawled over to the edge of the rock. Mama was in front of their hut, her head of wild hair thrown back and her arms waving. She was yelling at Uncle Bujiko.

Shida sighed and turned to begin her climb down the kopje, but as her eyes glanced over the round, granite surface, the same feeling of peace from her dream that morning settled over her.

Images of huge kopjes, formed of boulders stacked one on top of the other like a pyramid, flashed in Shida's mind. All around the pyramid was water, water stretching as far as the eye could see. "That's where I was," Shida said to herself. In her dream, she had been on the Sukuma pyramid that Babu spoke of. It had been like the river in Litongo, but a river that went in all directions, forever. Shida felt her body relax. The place of her ancestors. They had been strong and she could be, too. Shida straightened her back and cracked her neck.

She slid on her stomach over the rock face and lowered herself down to the dirt yard. When she reached the front of the hut, Mama was there, squatting in the yard next to Uncle Bujiko, pulling at her hair and groaning.

"We're ruined," Mama said.

Shida glared at her mother. What could she be worried about now? All the cattle were rounded up and returned to their corrals.

"Your father's cow is gone, Shida."

"Milembe?" Shida said.

"The old *mganga* told us to take care of that cow, Shida.

Now your father's spirit will haunt us forever."

Shida felt her heart race. "But all the other cows are here. Milembe can't be lost."

Mama looked up at Shida. Her face was smeared with dirt. "She's gone."

Milembe, their precious cow, had joined them two years ago when their tomato crops in Litongo had begun to fail. Mama had blamed Shida night and day when the plants' leaves wilted into brown, crackly skeletons before their fruit even developed. Babu must have taken pity on Shida, because he finally offered two chickens to the *mganga* in hopes that the old medicine man would be able to meet with Mama and offer her a real explanation for her tomatoes' failure.

Shida remembered that time. Mama had insisted that Shida join her and so they walked along the Litongo river, past several expansive compounds, until they reached the *mganga's* home. When they arrived, the old man was standing on top of a gently rising kopje. His youngest wife, dressed in pretty blue *kitenge*, gestured for Mama and Shida to be quiet. The *mganga* was finishing his morning ritual. He broke a dried cow pie in four and turned to throw quarters of the desiccated manure to the four corners of his compound. Shida stared. He had to be doing something wise — everyone agreed he could communicate with the ancestors — but why a cow pie?

The old man hobbled down from his rock mound, leaning onto his gnarled walking stick with one hand and gripping his tattered straw hat with the other. He greeted Mama and pointed them toward the outside of his hut.

"He'll want you to break a stem from that plant over there," his wife said. She pointed to a spindly plant with light green shoots. Shida had played with this kind of plant before, breaking the stems and squeezing out their sticky white juice.

Mama and Shida snapped off stems and the man mumbled.

"Spit on the stem and then stick it behind one of your ears," his wife said.

Mama and Shida obeyed and perched on two stools, less than a foot off the ground. The *mganga* sat down in a cowhide chair and shook a pair of dried gourds, whose seeds rattled as he sang. The shaking went on for a long time, long enough for Shida's thoughts to wander. She scanned the old man's yard, admiring his many papaya trees. She wondered if perhaps she and Grace could convince Uncle Bujiko to ask his cotton traders for a pair of gourds like the medicine man's.

When the old man's chanting finally finished, he stared at Mama. "The child's father —" he tilted his head toward Shida " — his spirit is unhappy. He's been dishonored. You must appease the spirit so that he'll leave you alone."

Shida wiggled on her stool, almost toppling it over. Had the *mganga* really talked to Father?

"In order to appease his spirit," the *mganga* said, "you must name a cow for him and place a bell around the cow's neck. Then he'll leave you alone."

Shida shrunk back on her stool. Did they really want Father to leave them alone? Shida hadn't been aware of Father's presence, but she had wondered about him. Was he handsome? What had he liked about Mama?

"But we don't have a cow," Mama snapped.

"I can't help you with that." The *mganga* pushed himself up on his walking stick and shuffled into the shade of his hut.

The whole walk home, Mama complained about the old man and his bad divination. "How could we — a widowed woman and single young girl — ever have a cow?"

But when they got back to Babu's compound, Mama went into the old man's hut to speak with her father. After a good while, Babu came out and hobbled toward the corral, pointing at a beautiful black cow with a white stripe that ran the length of its entire body. "We'll call her Milembe, the same name as your dead husband, in honor of his spirit," Babu said.

The next day, Mama strung a small metal bell onto a black string and tied it around the cow's neck. Shida could see Mama talking to the cow and moved closer until she could make out a few words. "There you go, Milembe," Mama said. "Be good to us."

"Shida, listen to me!" The sound of Uncle Bujiko's voice snapped Shida out of her memories.

She looked up at her uncle. His eyes looked puffy from lack of sleep. People said he was so determined to make Njia Panda into President Nyerere's best *ujamaa* village that he even went out to work in the village's communal fields at night.

"Shida, go look for your mother's cow. Then maybe she'll stop whining." He glared down at Mama, who was still rocking on the ground.

"May I take Grace?" Shida said.

Uncle Bujiko grimaced. Cows were the most valuable possession a Sukuma could own. Uncle Bujiko would probably prefer to send Shida with a boy cousin. But he nodded. "Take Grace, but be sure you come back with that cow."

An hour later, Shida and Grace were trudging up the rise in the road that led down to the school and clinic, where Old and New Njia Panda met.

When they reached the top of the hill, Grace stopped. She pointed down to the schoolyard, where a short, stout man was leading a herd of cows off the road. "Teacher Karakola!" The name unwound slowly from Grace's lips.

Teacher Karakola turned the corner of the school building, following his herd of cows. The girls ran down the hill to the schoolyard. When they reached the flamboyant tree, they slowed to a walk, taking deep, slow breaths as they rounded the school building. Teacher Karakola's cows were circling a wall of thick shrubs. Shida sprinted over to a hole in the wall of plants and watched Teacher Karakola lead the last of the cows into a thorny cattle corral.

"Look," Grace whispered. She pointed to the corner of the corral farthest from the teacher. A black cow's head popped over the side of the brambles, and then ducked back into the pack of other animals. "That's Milembe, isn't it?"

Shida squinted at the mass of heads bobbing up and down in the corral. "That cow didn't have a white stripe, did she?"

Grace shoved her hand over Shida's mouth.

On the other side of the plant wall, Teacher Karakola yawned and pushed the last bramble in place.

Shida felt sticky sap from the wall of plants she had been gripping run down one of her arms. She wiped her hands on her dress and watched Teacher Karakola walk toward his house. He was still yawning. Had he been up in the middle of the night, opening corrals? But Shida was suddenly distracted by a glint of light from the corral wall. Grace must have seen it, too, because she flinched.

There, hanging on the side of the corral, was a collar of long black string with a tiny bell, just like the one Milembe had worn.

Chapter 7

Wisdom is like a baobab tree; no one individual can embrace it.
— *Togolese proverb*

"It's him. He must have stolen Milembe," Grace whispered.

Teacher Karakola was still just on the other side of the thick wall of plants that separated the schoolyard from his hut and corral.

Shida squinted at her cousin. "But other people put charms around their cows' necks. How can we be sure *he* stole Milembe?"

"Teacher Karakola isn't a Sukuma, Shida!" Grace said. "That black string and bell is a Sukuma charm."

Shida began to nod, but something moved out of the corner of her eye and her head snapped up.

Standing right beside them, looming wide, was Teacher

Karakola. His eyes narrowed as he bent down to snatch up a stick.

For a second, Shida's body refused to move — even her lungs froze — but then she and Grace were running across the dirt schoolyard, their bare feet kicking up red flamboyant blossoms as they tried to stretch their arms and legs farther and farther away from the schoolyard.

"Get out of here!" Teacher Karakola's voice surged through the air behind them, like lightning on a hot night. His stick hissed as it cut through the air.

"Girls don't belong here at school on Saturdays . . . or ever!"

Shida and Grace ran home to tell Babu what they had seen. The old man listened, but said little. Shida could see the tiredness in the saggy skin under his eyes.

"Don't worry about the cow, my children. I'll find out what's gone wrong with her. I'll also talk to both of your teachers about welcoming girls at school. Rest your minds."

Shida tried to push the sounds of Teacher Karakola's shouts out of her thoughts, but an eerie feeling followed her the rest of that day. Why would Teacher Karakola, a man chosen to teach in this new *ujamaa* school, try to sabotage half of the village? If Shida's people weren't here, he would be out of a job. Besides, wouldn't he want to contribute to Nyerere's vision? Maybe he didn't want girls in the school — lots of people didn't. They thought girls should be at home learning to cook and farm and follow instructions so they could become good wives. But if Teacher Karakola didn't want girls at school, why didn't he just target the families of his few female students? Why all the people of Litongo?

✗✗✗✗✗✗✗✗✗✗✗✗✗✗✗✗

That evening, when Shida went to gather the laundry she had laid out to dry on the rocks behind her house, she couldn't find her yellow dress. She couldn't imagine anyone wanting to steal the faded garment with its ripped hem. There had been days in Litongo when Shida had tried to lose the dress, letting it float away down the river with the dirty wash water. But it had only sunk to the sandy river bottom and shone up at her — a ripply yellow blob that couldn't be ignored.

Though the dress didn't turn up, the cow did. On Sunday morning Milembe was there in the cattle corral — without her black string and bell charm, but there nonetheless. No one could explain her return and so no one said anything. Instead, when neighbors walked by Babu's compound, they swung wide out to the other side of the road, as if walking too close to Babu's cattle corral might bring them bad fortune.

✗✗✗✗✗✗✗✗✗✗✗✗✗✗✗✗

On Monday, just as Babu had instructed, Shida and Grace headed out to school with Furaha in tow. When the road reached the edge of the schoolyard, Furaha spotted Teacher Karakola walking around the corner of the schoolhouse. She threw herself down in the dirt and pursed her lips in a pout. "I won't go, Grace!"

"Furaha, Babu promised us he'd talk to your teacher."

Furaha pulled her knees up to her chest and covered her head with her hands. "I hate my teacher and besides, I wanted to wear my pink blouse today."

Grace rolled her eyes. "Furaha, I spent all morning looking for your blouse. You know that. What else do you want me to do?"

"She's missing clothes, too?" Shida said.

"Yes," Grace groaned. "She probably just took it outside to show to one of her little friends, and then one of them walked away with it."

"Well, Furaha," Shida said, "it's your turn to have class under the flamboyant tree. You do know what people say about a flamboyant flower falling on the head of a little girl?"

Furaha peeked out at Shida from behind one of her hands.

"People say that if a flamboyant flower falls on the head of a little girl, she'll be beautiful forever, and I know it's true, because that's exactly what happened to the nurse."

Furaha studied Shida's face, half smiling and half grimacing.

Shida smiled. "I'm not lying, Furaha. I don't care if you go to school, but I don't think there are any flamboyant trees near your house."

Furaha pushed herself to her feet, still eyeing Shida. She turned to look at her other cousins playing under the flamboyant tree. "I'm going to play."

"Good," Shida said.

As Shida and Grace hurried into the classroom, Grace turned to her cousin. "That story about flamboyant trees isn't true, is it?"

"No." Shida laughed. "But maybe for Furaha it will be."

That morning, after a lesson on the sounds of letters, Teacher Mrefu asked Shida and Grace to stay behind during recess. Gervas pranced toward the door with an enormous grin on his wide face. "*Kwa heri,*" he mouthed over his shoulder — the Swahili words for "goodbye." Shida scowled back at him, but inside she felt herself shaking. Perhaps Teacher Mrefu had decided not to admit the girls to the school after all. What would Babu say if Shida and all of her female cousins were sent away from school? Hadn't educating girls been a specific part of Nyerere's plan?

Shida squeezed up against Grace on their wooden bench and Grace gripped Shida's hand. If they had to leave school, they'd miss learning reading and math, as well as lessons about diseases and farming. Mama would probably start talking about finding Shida a husband again.

"I have some concerns I want to discuss with you," Teacher Mrefu said. "But first we'll wait for Teacher Karakola to come with his girl students."

Shida kept her eyes down and dug with her thumbnail into the crusty residue of sap on the skirt of her green dress.

"Teacher Karakola, what is the news of your morning?" Teacher Mrefu said.

Teacher Karakola sidestepped through the narrow classroom door. "Good," he grumbled.

A line of little girls led by Furaha scurried into the room. They squeezed all eight of their small bodies onto two benches.

"Girls," Teacher Mrefu said, looming over them. "Teacher Karakola and I have an important announcement to make. This government school is one of the first schools in a *ujamaa* village set up according to the plan of our respected President Nyerere. We're a model to other villages in Tanzania . . ."

Shida closed her eyes and sighed.

"As a model to the nation, we have many responsibilities and a great need to keep up our reputation . . ."

Shida had heard this story before. In order to be traditional and correct, the school would have to be only for boys.

". . . And so it is very important that we make this

school education available to both boys *and* girls."

Shida looked up, craning her head to see the tall man's face. He was smiling.

"So we can stay?" The words burst out of Shida's mouth before she even realized she was speaking.

"Hush, you awful child!" Teacher Karakola said.

"Please, Teacher Karakola," Teacher Mrefu said. "The girl has reason to celebrate. Ours is an African nation dedicated to educating not only its boys, but also its girls. That is something to be proud of.

"An elder from the new section of our village has visited us and mentioned that some of you have faced abuse from people here in the school." Teacher Mrefu looked down toward Teacher Karakola, who was balanced on a stool in the corner. "As head teacher of this school, I am here to ask you all to work hard and to accept challenges, but also to let me know when you face abuse. Please know that you're all welcome here, always."

That afternoon, Teacher Mrefu started class by writing the word *agriculture* on the board. Shida flipped open her notebook and copied the curvy lines of the letters he had written. She drew a plant next to the foreign-looking word to remind herself what the notes were about.

For the next hour, Teacher Mrefu talked about farming methods, some of which were familiar, like the fact that crops grow faster when animal manure is mixed into the soil. Other topics were completely new to Shida, like the idea that crop failure caused by insects, or something the teacher called "fungus," could be controlled.

"Sir," a boy in the class asked, "do these insects or this thing you call fungus come because of a curse?"

"Insects and fungi are living creatures. They must eat, just like you and me, so there doesn't need to be a curse for them to start eating crops." Teacher Mrefu drew a bug taking a bite out of a leaf. Shida admired his perfect white lines on the blackboard and tried to copy them into her book.

"The good thing is that we can learn what these insects and fungi don't like," Teacher Mrefu said. "Many of these pests will go away if you sprinkle ashes on the leaves of your crops. Some can be eaten by other insects that do not hurt the crops."

Shida's face scrunched up. Could it really be true? If she and Mama had sprinkled ashes on their tomatoes, then the crops would have survived?

"In cases where ashes or other beneficial insects don't work, there are chemicals that can be applied," Teacher Mrefu said. "The government has given our village some of these chemicals to use on our shared village crops, but we have to be careful with these chemicals, because too much of them can actually kill the crops."

Shida scribbled pictures of everything they learned until she had a page full of neat dark lines on clean paper. When Teacher Mrefu was done with his explanations, he took the class out into a small garden plot between his hut and the schoolyard. He pointed out a line of pepper plants whose leaves were pocked with small holes. Shida ran over to a thorny, flat-topped acacia tree at the edge of the garden plot and carefully propped her notebook and Grace's next to its trunk before running back to join the group. Hunching over the plants, the students hunted for insects, which they caught and showed to Teacher Mrefu. Within ten minutes, they had a collection of worms and bugs, some of which Teacher Mrefu said were good for the plants and the soil, and others which he said were the cause of the holes. He showed the students a pile of ashes he had collected from nearby homes, and the students each were assigned five pepper plants to dust in ashes.

Shida and Grace chose the plants down at the farthest end of the line and gently covered them in soot. Shida was careful not to lose too much of the ash to the ground and instead dusted each leaf, imagining each green shoot as one of her patients who needed to be healed. When she was done, she grabbed Grace's hand and skipped back to the tree where she had left their notebooks. The boys had already run off into the schoolyard — the leaves on many of their plants looked bare and exposed from lack of properly applied soot.

"I took lots of notes so that we can remember all that we learned today," Shida said. She and Grace snatched up their notebooks, but the familiar lump of Shida's pencil near her notebook's spine was missing. Shida scanned the ground and found her pencil sticking out of the dry earth. She pulled it out. The tip was broken. Shida flipped the notebook open and on the page where she expected to see her drawings of insects, plants and powder, there was a messy sketch of a round boy in shorts, holding a long stick.

Gervas.

Over his head was a roof, which extended into a long building. Underneath was scratched a word: "SKOOL."

Below the boy was a girl in a dress with the same spotted, bumblebee pattern as Shida's green dress. The girl had a straight face, no stick, and no roof over her head. Underneath the empty ground where she stood were written the words "NO SKOOL."

"That idiot!" Shida jumped to her feet. "I'll get him." She began to run toward the schoolyard, but Grace's long arms held her back.

"What're you doing, Shida? You can't beat him up. You're a girl, and it's not like he's your younger brother or someone you're allowed to hit."

Shida jerked the full weight of her body forward, trying to free herself. This was ridiculous. Shida didn't care if she got in trouble for beating him up.

"Shida! You're a girl. It doesn't matter what Teacher Karakola or Babu think. If you beat up Gervas, we'll be chased out of this village."

Shida stopped struggling. Grace was right. "I wish he'd fall into a pit of biting *siafu* ants and get eaten alive," Shida said.

Grace laughed. "Yes, but if he fell into a pit of *siafu* ants, he'd have to take off his clothes to get them off. Then we'd have to see him naked before he was dead."

Shida groaned. "I don't even want to think about that. Let's go tell Teacher Mrefu what he did."

×××××××××××××××××

When Teacher Mrefu had finally called the other students back to class for their last hour of lessons, he stood at the front of the room and stared down at each of the students. Shida noticed him grit his teeth as his eyes settled on Gervas.

"Young man, do you have anything to admit?" His voice was calm, but stern.

"No." Gervas squeaked and seemed to be trying not to laugh.

Teacher Mrefu held up Shida's notebook and flipped through the marred pages. "Did you do this?"

"Yes," Gervas said. A nervous chuckle slipped out of him. Some of the other boys in the room snickered.

"Stop laughing!" Teacher Mrefu boomed. "There's no excuse for this kind of behavior. Girls are just as welcome in this school as boys, and if I see any other mean-spirited behavior from any of you, you'll be suspended from school for a week." He walked over to Gervas and looked down at him. "Gervas, you've already been warned. Go fetch me a stick from the schoolyard."

Shida gasped. So Gervas would be beaten.

"Gervas, go . . . fetch . . . a stick . . . from . . . the . . . yard!" Teacher Mrefu ground each word between his teeth as he spoke.

Shida gulped and turned just in time to see Gervas shove his desk forward. She and Grace jumped up as it crashed into their bench.

Gervas charged across the classroom and turned around in the doorway. He glared at Teacher Mrefu. "I won't get the stick. You can't tell me what to do. You can't beat me." Gervas looked down and shook his head.

When he looked up, there were tears running down his round cheeks. "You're not even Sukuma. You're just a foreigner. My father says that if you weren't here, if this were a proper Sukuma school, then there'd be no girls. These girls' families wouldn't have invaded our village!" He turned and ran toward the road.

Shida and her classmates stared at the blinding light of the midday sun that shone through the empty doorframe.

Teacher Mrefu stood quietly, tall as a giraffe, but anger flashed in his eyes as he stared out the door. "You're excused for the day," he said.

Outside, a pigeon cooed, but no one inside the classroom stirred.

Teacher Mrefu's lips bulged over his clenched teeth. "I said you were excused, all of you! Now go!"

Chapter 8

Rain does not fall on one roof alone.
— *Cameroonian proverb*

"I'll just rinse these pots and then come," Grace said. She was squatting in front of a pile of Mama's dirty dishes outside Shida's hut.

Shida snatched up her pail and jogged down the road leading to the pump. The pounding of her feet felt stiff, but Shida stretched her arms and legs longer as she ran. She enjoyed the burning in her lungs, as if she were melting away the tension of the day.

At the last bend in the road before the pump, Shida squinted up toward the eucalyptus trees. Their silvery blue leaves swayed in the warm afternoon air. Something moved in their branches. Was that a kingfisher bird?

SMACK!

The full force of Shida's body collided with another. Bony arms, faded gray *kitenge* cloth, water, a clanging metal pail.

Shida rubbed her eyes. She lay on her back in the dirt, her heart thundering in her chest, one of her shins screaming with pain, and . . . a woman's shrill voice. Shida propped herself up on her elbows. Mama Malongo was stretched out in the road beside her.

Shida shivered. Of all the people to run into — a witch.

Mama Malongo met Shida's stare. Her eyes were red, just as all witches' eyes were supposed to be, and her hair looked just like Mama's — sticking out in knotty clumps — only Mama Malongo's was gray.

"Where were you running? Where were your eyes, young girl? You knocked me to the ground and spilled my pail of water." The old woman pushed her tired frame up off her bent knee. "That school certainly isn't doing you any good. No one's teaching you proper manners there. You're like bad fruit that's been left to rot on the ground. You don't even look where you run." As she spoke, Mama Malongo batted at her pail where it lay tipped over in the road, its last droplets of water seeping in the sand below.

Shida stumbled to her feet. "I'm sorry. I was . . . I wasn't looking."

"Well, of course you weren't looking!" Mama Malongo

stood up as straight as her hunched spine would allow and gripped her hip. It jutted out at a sharp angle under her ratty *kitenge* cloth. "You've lost my bucket of water and you've caused me pain in my hip."

"I'm sorry," Shida said. She picked up her own pail and shuffled backward, avoiding the old woman's stare.

"Pick up my pail and go collect water for me — three buckets worth."

Shida's brow furrowed. Three buckets? But Mama Malongo's red eyes glowed back at her.

Shida snatched up Mama Malongo's pail and ran toward the pump.

"Walk!" Mama Malongo screeched after her. "Is this what they teach you in school — to run with your eyes closed?"

Just as Shida was finishing filling Mama Malongo's pail, she heard feet pounding up the road behind her.

"Shida!" Grace gasped for air. "What happened with Mama Malongo? She was mumbling your name when I passed her on the road."

Shida stopped pumping. The gush of water slowed to a trickle. "I ran into her."

Grace's face dropped. "You ran into Mama Malongo? Shida, people say she's been complaining about girls going to school. She didn't need another excuse to start causing us trouble."

"I know, Grace, but now she needs her three buckets of water, and you know she'll curse me if I don't deliver them." Shida lifted her own bucket on top of her head and then she squatted down. Straining to keep her spine straight, she lifted Mama Malongo's bucket onto her hip. "I should get going on my first trip. You get started filling Mama's barrel."

Grace's hand met Shida's chest. "No, Shida. Don't be silly. I'm coming with you. Just wait for me to fill my pail."

Thick trees bordered the narrow path leading to Mama Malongo's compound. Shida had to shuffle sideways with her full bucket on her head and Mama Malongo's on her hip.

"Should I take one of your buckets for a — ?" Grace stumbled into Shida, who had suddenly stopped.

"Look down," Shida whispered.

The late afternoon wind was whipping eucalyptus leaves and sand into a funnel just up the trail. Both girls stared as it settled at Shida's feet.

Shida gulped. Every Sukuma knew that a pile of leaves and sand blown into a path was the sign of a witch's recent passage.

"Come on, Shida," Grace said. "Let's deliver this water quickly and get out of here."

The two girls hurried down the path, studying the

shadowy ground and the dark lines of trees beside them. Shida strained to keep her grip on the bucket sliding off her hip.

Whoo, ooh. Something called down from the treetops.

"What was that?" Shida turned to Grace.

"I don't know." Grace's face was long and serious.

Whoo, ooh . . . Whoo, ooh . . . Whoo, ooh.

"She's sent an owl to listen to us!" Shida ran down the trail, water sloshing onto her arms and face. She didn't care what was waiting behind a tree or under a leaf ahead of them — all she wanted to do was to get rid of this water and run home before Mama Malongo or her owl placed a curse on one of them. The path curved through dense trees and opened up on a clearing in the woods. Shida's eyes darted around the compound. There were miniature structures all over the yard — twigs and bark leaning together into sloppily constructed houses the size of Shida's hand.

"Spirit houses!" Grace gasped.

Shida felt her stomach turn. Good people might build one or two spirit houses to welcome their ancestors, but no one ever built this many spirit houses. "This is really bad magic, Grace," Shida said.

But Grace was already pulling Shida across the yard, tiptoeing around the tiny houses. Shida kept her eyes on the ground, ready for something to jump out at them.

They reached a clay water barrel. Grace dumped her

pail of water into the barrel, and Shida emptied hers, but as she raised Mama Malongo's bucket, Grace put up her hand.

"Listen," she said.

Groaning came from under a triangle of propped-up corrugated metal next to them. "This place is a curse. Girls go bad in that school . . . old people are left to live under two pieces of metal. Oh, yes . . . the farms, you say . . . which land did they choose for the old witch to farm? *Ehh*, the land farthest away from this cramped village. *Ehh*, the old woman will walk more than an hour just to get to her field."

Shida looked up. "Let's get out of here," she whispered.

But Grace was still staring at the metal tent. "It's true what she's saying though. People like my father got fields right next to their huts, but people like these old widows, they have to walk half a morning to get to their fields."

"Maybe it's not fair, but she's a witch, Grace." Shida's panic made her whisper sound more like a hiss. She poured Mama Malongo's bucket of water into the clay barrel in a thin, quiet stream, picked up their two pails, careful not to bump their metal sides together, and took her cousin's hand. As they stepped around little rooftops of moss and walls of tree bark, Grace seemed to drag more and more heavily on Shida.

At the edge of the clearing, Shida whipped around.

"Come on, Grace. You're not feeling sorry for her, are you? Mama Malongo's crazy. Who do you think she was talking to in there? An owl?"

Grace glared at her cousin. "She wasn't talking to an owl, Shida! She was talking to herself inside the hut that no one bothered to build for her."

"She's a witch, Grace!"

"Maybe she is, or maybe she's just an old woman no one treats nicely. If she's a witch, people made her that way."

"Maybe, but look at all these spirit houses," Shida said. "She deserves to be called a witch."

"Just like your mama?"

Shida gasped. She felt as if she had fallen from a tall papaya tree and had the wind knocked out of her. How could Grace say something like that? Mama was different.

"Come on," Grace said. She took Shida's hand and pulled her up the trail. They stumbled through the dark woods, tripping over tree roots. When they arrived at the road, Grace stopped. "The pile of leaves is gone."

"Yes," Shida said. She turned to look back down the trail toward Mama Malongo's house. Maybe Grace was right. Maybe . . .

Shida shivered.

"Are you okay?" Grace said.

"Look!" Shida's voice squeaked.

Grace squinted down the dark trail. There, hanging from a branch at eye level, a few feet in from the road, was a black string with a small metal bell on it, just like the one that had hung outside Teacher Karakola's corral. Just like the string and bell that had disappeared from their cow Milembe.

Chapter 9

He who learns, teaches.
— Ethiopian proverb

The two girls stood on the edge of the road, squinting into the shadows of Mama Malongo's trail.

"Maybe *he* put the bell there," Grace said.

"Teacher Karakola?" Shida said. "He's not even a Sukuma, Grace. He doesn't know Mama Malongo's a witch."

"Shida, no one knows if Mama Malongo's a witch."

"Oh, stop it, Grace. You saw those spirit houses. Mama Malongo's trying to communicate with ancestors. You heard her inside her hut. She called herself a witch. She said she hates living here. So it's perfect for her to curse us all in Njia Panda. If the village decides to move back to Litongo, then she can, too."

"I guess so, but how were there two bells?" Grace said. "Milembe only had one."

Shida nodded. Grace was right. The bell was a Sukuma charm made for cows — Teacher Karakola wasn't Sukuma and Mama Malongo didn't have cows, so neither of them would have had a charm of their own like this.

"We've got to talk to Babu," Grace said.

The two girls ran back to Babu's hut, but just as Shida was about to duck through his door, one of her aunts came out, carrying Babu's cowhide sleeping mat.

"Where's Babu?" Shida said. She felt panic rise in her chest once again.

"Everything's fine, Sister." Shida's aunt smiled. "Your Babu's just staying in a village hut out near the collective cotton farms this week. The work's getting intense and he wants to be there to help direct the men and women. He'll sleep there until Saturday to save his energy."

"Saturday?" Grace said.

"Yes, Saturday." The woman laughed. "I know you love your Babu, but you two should be able to survive five days without him."

The girls thanked their aunt and walked around to the other side of the cattle corral. One of their young cousins was herding Babu's cattle into the ring of thorny brambles.

"Where are the collective fields?" Shida shouted over the din of the cattle.

"About an hour away," Grace said, "but if we go there, Babu will be surrounded by people. We won't get a chance to talk to him. I don't think we have a choice, Shida. I think we'll have to wait until Saturday."

Shida groaned. "You're right, but five days, Grace! Five days will take forever."

<hr />

"I'd like to introduce you to Nurse Goldfilda." Teacher Mrefu was standing in front of the class, gesturing toward his desk. The plump woman sat tall in his chair.

Shida sat up on the bench she shared with Grace, making her back extra long and tall, just as the nurse did.

"Thank you for inviting me, Teacher Mrefu. I see some faces here I recognize." The nurse nodded toward Shida, then marched up to the chalkboard and wrote a word on the board. "Does anyone know what this word means?" She turned to the class.

The uneven legs of Gervas's desk tapped back and forth on the compact dirt floor behind Shida.

"The students are just learning to read, despite their age," Teacher Mrefu said. "In fact, some of them are still learning to speak Swahili, so I've been trying to talk slowly, if you'd be willing to do the same."

"Oh, of course," said the nurse. "Pardon me. I forget they've been in school for less than a week." She turned to the class. "The word is *malaria*."

The nurse had used this word in Litongo. Malaria was what she called the sickness that came with aching joints, headache, and fever. Shida used steam from boiled *mamihigo* bark to treat patients with fever, and the nurse used white pills that made the patient's ears ring.

"Malaria is spread by mosquitoes," the nurse said. "There's a particular mosquito called the anopheles. This female mosquito pricks the skin of someone with malaria to drink that person's blood, but when she drinks the blood, she also takes in some of the malaria parasites."

Shida raised her hand. "What are parasites?"

Her bench jumped with a kick. Gervas snickered.

"That's a great question, Shida." The nurse smiled, showing off her beautiful white teeth. "Parasites are things that live off of something else. In this case, they're like miniscule insects that get into this female mosquito, and then when she goes to drink the blood of another person, she leaves some of the parasites behind. The problem is that once these parasites get into a person's blood, they multiply. This usually takes about two weeks, which means the person will get very sick two weeks after he's bitten."

Shida copied down the curvy lines for the word *malaria* as the nurse spoke. She drew two people with a mosquito between them and a trail of little bugs connecting them. Shida grimaced as she finished the drawing. She sure could use more practice drawing. The mosquito looked like a flying person with a beak, but it didn't matter. Shida wouldn't forget what any of it meant. Several children in Litongo had died from high fever and achy joints — her patient, Baby Lewanga, had almost been one of them. The medicine men always declared that these children's deaths were caused by curses, bad medicine, or unhappy ancestors, but perhaps malaria also had something to do with it.

"Protecting yourself against mosquitoes is very important," the nurse said. "Fortunately, the anopheles mosquito only comes out at sunup and sundown, so you only need to be careful at those times."

Sunup and sundown? Maybe that was Baby Lewanga's problem. He had been getting sick every couple of months for the last year. Villagers were certain he was cursed, but maybe he just spent too much time playing outside in the evening.

"I hope none of you say 'yes,'" the nurse said, "but have any of you had brothers or sisters who died with fevers?"

Five students raised their hands.

"Well, it's quite possible some of them died of malaria."

━━━━━━━━━━━━━

"Shida, let's go." Grace was yanking at Shida's dirty green sleeve. The nurse had stopped talking and the lesson was over.

Shida looked up to watch her male classmates file out of the room for recess. She closed her notebook and followed Grace toward the doorway where Teacher Mrefu was talking with the nurse.

"I'm sorry," Nurse Goldfilda said to Teacher Mrefu. "I just need to catch up with this young woman quickly." She turned to Shida. "What is your news, little sister?"

"I'm well, thank you."

The nurse smiled. "Have you been continuing with your healing work here in Njia Panda?"

"No," Shida said. "I mean, no one has come for my help since we moved. My mother and I came to Njia Panda late, just last week."

"Well, if you're not busy with your own work, would you like to come help me with mine?"

A huge hiccup rattled Shida's body. She felt her face grow hot.

"Yes, she'd love to come," Grace answered for Shida. "How about after school?"

The nurse smiled. "That would be fine. In fact, if you can come every Tuesday, I'd be grateful. I'll be waiting for you today, little sister."

"Thank you," Shida said. She took one more glimpse at the beautiful woman in her shining white uniform, and then she felt her arm being yanked. Grace pulled her out the door.

<hr />

Shida took a deep breath as she walked up the clinic stairs

that afternoon. She cracked the open door and peeked in. The front room had two wooden benches resting on a perfectly smooth cement floor. A woman sat on one bench, hunched over her toddler. She mopped the shivering child's brow.

"Mama Lewanga, is that you?" Shida said.

The woman turned, and her tense face relaxed for a minute. "Shida, I came looking for you. Lewanga has the sickness again. He's hot, but he's also shivering. People say the bad spirit that possessed him has followed us here. He needs some of your medicine, Shida."

The curtain blocking the doorway at the opposite side of the room swung open, and Nurse Goldfilda appeared. "Oh, Shida. You've come at a good time. I could use your help." She hurried over to Baby Lewanga and squatted in front of him. The boy's head was flopped to the side, but when his eyes met Nurse Goldfilda's, he squirmed to turn away from her.

"Please calm the child," the nurse said in Swahili, looking up at Mama Lewanga. "I have to prick his finger for blood, and I can't have him moving like this."

When Baby Lewanga's eyes caught the glint of the sharp instrument in the nurse's hand, he started screaming.

Mama Lewanga clutched him to her chest and shook her head. "Don't do it. You can't hurt my baby. He can't cry. When he cries, the bad spirit takes over his body."

Shida stared at them. Baby Lewanga was sicker than she'd ever seen him. Shida didn't blame Mama Lewanga for getting upset. With her other two children gone, Baby Lewanga was all Mama Lewanga had left.

"Can I try?" The words slipped out of Shida's mouth before she even realized what she was saying. "You need to get some blood to look for the malaria bugs, right?"

"Exactly," the nurse said.

Shida placed her hands on Mama Lewanga's shoulders and began speaking in their Sukuma language. "It's okay, *Mayu*. We want to help your baby. He's very sick and we need you to help us. This nurse here has to test his blood for a sickness called malaria and then she'll know what medicine to give him. The medicine's very strong, but if she finds that it's what he needs, I believe it will work even better than the *mamihigo* tea. The nurse gave it to me once in Litongo. Please help us, *Mayu*."

Mama Lewanga shuddered, but she nodded her tear-stained face. She loosened her grip on Baby Lewanga and turned his head with both of her hands toward Shida.

"Hello, Baraka."

Baby Lewanga's face relaxed and he closed his eyes.

"Good boy, good Baraka." Shida took the child's tiny hand in her own and ran her calloused fingers up and down his smooth arm. It radiated heat.

"You'll need to poke his fingertip with this tool in order

to draw blood." The nurse whispered in Shida's ear. "Once the blood bubbles up, then wipe it on this glass slide. We have to do it quickly. The child looks very sick."

Shida took a deep breath and concentrated on the boy's tiny face. "Baraka, you're a big boy now, aren't you? I need you to help me, Baraka. I'm going to pinch your finger and it'll hurt, but we'll make you better. Can you help me, Baraka?"

The little boy's face convulsed with a shiver, but he opened his eyes and blinked once.

Shida eased the sharp instrument down onto the child's fingertip. Her arms began to shake. She'd never caused anyone to bleed.

"That's it, Shida," the nurse whispered.

Mama Lewanga's sniffling filled the room.

"You can do it," the nurse said. "This boy needs you now, Shida."

Shida gritted her teeth and clenched the metal tool. She forced her hand to press the sharp point into Baby Lewanga's plump fingertip. The little boy flinched, but even when a shining red bubble of blood appeared on his fingertip, he didn't cry.

Shida wiped the blood onto the glass slide and exhaled. "Good boy, Baraka, good boy." She gripped the little boy's head and placed her forehead against his. "You did it, Baraka. We're going to make you better."

Twenty minutes later, the nurse emerged from the back room with tablets and a glass of water in her hand. Shida was holding the little boy's limp body in her lap. She had wrapped the child in wet towels, but his forehead still radiated heat. Mama Lewanga was hunched over him, studying his face.

"He has malaria," the nurse said. "There are many parasites in his blood. We'll have to give him these tablets right away. They'll kill the parasites, but they'll make his ears ring and they might make him feel like vomiting. Even if he feels sick, Mama Lewanga, he must take the tablets regularly for the next three days. After he gets better, I want you to come back so that we can talk about how to prevent this kind of sickness."

Mama Lewanga knew as much Swahili as Shida, but Shida still translated the nurse's instructions into Sukuma.

When Shida was done speaking, Mama Lewanga looked up. "Do you think this is good medicine, Shida? Is the nurse saying my son's possessed?" She spoke in Sukuma.

"No, she doesn't believe your son's possessed." Shida looked directly into the woman's eyes. "The nurse might even have some ideas to prevent him from getting sick again, but right now he needs this medicine. I know it'll make him better. But if you like, I'll also make some *mamihigo* tea for him."

Mama Lewanga glanced down at her boy. She looked back up at Shida. "Alright, Shida. I trust you." She pinched Baby Lewanga's cheeks open, placed a pill on his tongue and held the glass of water to his lips.

The boy swallowed.

Chapter 10

From the word of an elder is derived a bone.
— *Burundian proverb*

When Saturday morning finally arrived, Shida felt like an overripe papaya, ready to burst. Before sunrise, she had already filled their compound's water barrel and begun to scrub last night's dishes with sand. As she worked, all she could think of were the stories she would tell Babu when he finally settled into his cowhide chair that night.

"We'll go to our new farm plot today." Mama appeared in the door of their hut. "Your grandfather gave me some cassava tubers last week. They're probably the only plant that will survive so far out from the village without regular water."

Shida's hand froze on the pot she was scrubbing. A

slurry of ash and water dripped onto her feet. Was Mama serious? She hadn't done any physical work for more than two months.

"I told Bujiko to send one of his boys to take us there," Mama said. "The plot's so far away, we couldn't possibly find it ourselves."

Shida shook her head and went back to scrubbing. So, they'd farm today, on the day when she most wanted to be home to greet Babu.

Uncle Bujiko's son Kulwa arrived at the house at mid-morning. He walked up to Mama and, without a word, continued on behind Babu's hut out to a cluster of fields Shida had yet to explore. The tiny boy walked with his hands in the pockets of his nice new khaki shorts. He swung his right foot out with each step, just like his father.

"What an awful child." Mama was hurrying behind Shida to catch up. "Imagine, ten years old and already too grown up to greet his elders. At least he's not as sickly and weak as his father was when he was this age."

Kulwa stopped in the middle of the first field. Neat rows of maize in already-watered wells of soil stretched out on either side of them. "This is Babu's field. It's big and near to the village because he's an important man, like my father."

Shida watched Mama's hands squeeze the handle of

the *jembe* hoe balanced on her shoulder. "Keep walking, Kulwa!" she said.

The three of them continued for over an hour across increasingly small and parched plots. When the sun had almost reached the middle of the sky, the little boy stopped in the ring of fields farthest from the village. Underneath their feet was an unweeded patch of parched earth staked out with four crooked wooden sticks.

"This is your plot. Father sent me to mark it for you. He didn't have time to do it himself."

Shida swung her *jembe* hoe down from her shoulder. The blade hit the dry soil with a loud smack and the little boy's eyes jumped to meet hers.

"Show me where we can find water, Kulwa," Shida said.

"There isn't any water here." Kulwa raised one of his tiny eyebrows just as Uncle Bujiko did when he was feeling proud. "Some of the men who have plots near Father dug a huge hole to collect rain water. Too bad you don't have important neighbors like Father to help you dig a hole."

Shida bent at the waist and stuck her face right in front of her cousin's. "I don't believe you ever greeted me as your elder today, Kulwa, so I see no need to listen to you."

The little boy stumbled backwards and tripped over Mama's legs where she had stretched out on the cracked earth. Kulwa squealed and scrambled to his feet, keeping his eyes on Mama.

Mama turned her head and spat, hitting one of his bare feet.

Kulwa screamed and jumped away.

Shida smiled. "Tell me one more thing before you go. Whose plot is this?" Shida pointed to the only plot that bordered hers and Mama's. It was also small, but at least it was one position closer to the village.

"It's Mama Malongo's plot," Kulwa said. He was backing away toward the village, his eyes still on Mama. "It's — "

"No, you don't need to say it," Shida said. "It's the witch's plot, right? So even the witch gets a better plot than . . ." Shida turned to look back at Mama. Her eyes were nearly closed and her chin rested on her collarbone.

"You may go, Kulwa," Shida said.

The little boy backed away across Mama Malongo's plot and then turned to run, bouncing through the waves of a heat mirage.

Shida turned to Mama. "Mama, please get up," Shida said. "We've got a lot of work to do if we're ever going to grow anything here." Shida grabbed her *jembe* hoe and began dragging its blade, scarring the soil with lines to mark their rows. When she got to the middle of the plot where Mama still sat, she crouched down in front of her mother.

Mama's eyes were closed.

Shida gritted her teeth and took a deep breath. She shoved her hands under the bony woman's arms and heaved

Mama up onto her knees.

Mama's eyes popped open and her face began to pinch into a scowl, but she stumbled to her feet.

Shida snatched up her hoe and continued scraping lines in the soil. "It's a good thing you thought of cassava, Mama. We won't be able to water out here at all. Now, we'll need big valleys and ridges of soil in case the rains are heavy. Here, I'll start digging in this corner, and you start over there."

Shida swung her *jembe* hoe into the hard-packed earth. It reverberated back, hardly making an indent. She raised it again and swung down with the full force of her body. *Thwack*. The blade cut into the dirt.

Thwack. There was an echo.

Shida looked up. Mama's blade was sunk deep into the ground. The frail woman heaved her body back and pulled up a big chunk of dirt.

That evening when Shida came running back from the fields, Babu was sitting in front of his hut, resting in his cowhide chair. He looked like he had never left. Shida fell down on her knees in front of the old man and greeted him in Sukuma. "*Ny'wadela*, Babu."

He waved her to her feet and smiled. "Oh, Daughter Shida, how good it is to see you. Come and sit."

Shida slid into the chair next to him and looked out

over the yard. The evening light had turned that rare color of golden red that made everything glow with warmth.

"Our brother sun is looking down on us kindly," Babu said. He gazed at Shida. "But your dress, my daughter. Has no one helped you with the clothes washing?"

Shida glanced down at her filthy dress. It was covered in dirt, soot stains, and dried starchy rice water. "I . . . my yellow dress disappeared, Babu. I laid it out on the rocks to dry last weekend, and after we discovered Milembe had returned, it was missing. I searched everywhere and it's gone." Shida paused, trying to decide what she should tell Babu next, but before she knew it the story of the whole week poured out of her. She told her grandfather everything about school and the two teachers, about Mama Malongo, about Nurse Goldfilda, and about their new farming plot.

"Sometimes I think Mama Malongo is an awful woman who put a curse on this village just to make all of us move back, and then I think about how people" — Shida glanced toward her hut — "how people call Mama a witch."

Babu ground the worn end of his walking stick into the packed earth between his feet. "You young people think very quickly. Sometimes this is a problem. Last time I saw you, you thought this teacher of yours, Karakola, I believe, had stolen your mother's cow. Now, you think Mama Malongo is responsible. What you tell me of the leaves forming a pile in the trail, we Sukuma believe this is a sign of a witch, and we also believe red eyes are the sign of witches. But eyes are often made red by cooking with fires fueled by dried cow manure."

Shida stared at her grandfather.

Babu studied Shida's face. "Who fuels their cooking fire with cow manure, young daughter?"

"Well, many people."

Babu raised his eyebrows.

"I guess Mama and I cook with cow dung sometimes, and so does Mama Gatambi, and I think I've seen Mama Malongo collecting dried cow pies. . . ." Shida's eyes widened. "I guess mostly poor widows cook with cow manure."

"Mmm," Babu hummed. "Red eyes might be the sign of a witch, but they also might be the sign of not having enough children to collect firewood."

Shida fiddled with the hem of her dress. "So that's why you help Mama Malongo when others call her a witch? You think she's just a poor widow like Mama?"

Babu rested his chin on his walking stick and looked out toward the corral. The cattle were finally growing quiet. "I don't know if she's a witch. We saw the owl fly back toward her house last weekend, but it may have been flying to another house as well. What I do know is she's alone and no one else helps her. It's important to help those who are alone. We Sukuma used to take good care of our neighbors — we understood one another as one extended family — but during the *wazungu*'s rule, we sometimes lost track of that tradition. Teacher Nyerere is asking us to remember that we are a people who have always worked for everyone's good; we are a people who do not forget those in need."

Shida's throat tightened. Babu certainly helped out Shida and Mama.

Happy shouts bounced across the yard from the road, and Shida and Babu turned to look at a pair of toddlers kicking a ball of bound maize husks through the sand. Shida squinted — the boy was Baby Lewanga.

"That's —" But when she turned to Babu, his wide, wrinkly grin told her he already knew.

"*Ehh*, my daughter," Babu said. "You've done well healing the young boy."

Shida ran to her hut and returned with her notebook from school. She pulled her chair up next to Babu's and flipped through each page, explaining her drawings.

"And this — " Shida turned a page in the notebook, revealing Gervas's angry drawings scowling up at her. She quickly flipped to the next page.

"What was that, my daughter?"

"Oh, nothing." She'd already complained enough.

Babu's bony fingers grasped the corner of the page. "There's never nothing in something. I want you to tell me everything about school."

Shida sighed. "I told you about the boy who gives us

trouble at school? He made this drawing to try to scare us away, and then when our teacher found out and scolded him, Gervas called Teacher Mrefu a foreigner and said that people like him are responsible for us *invading* his village."

"Invading, huh?" Babu stared off toward the trees. "Who is this boy's father?"

"Kifaro, I think."

Babu took a deep breath and leaned back in his chair. "*Ehh*, I thought so. Gervas's father was the old chief of Njia Panda. The man has many wives and many children. He lost his power to a council of elders when our country got its independence, so he's probably still upset about that, and about what Gervas calls the invasion of our people into Njia Panda."

"But we didn't *invade*, Babu!" Shida said.

"Oh, perhaps we did, or perhaps we were welcomed. Words are funny in that way. This move's been difficult on many people. All of us now have neighbors pushing up against our compounds. Some, like your mother and Mama Malongo, have to walk farther to farm. And . . . well, even people like me who were respected in Litongo don't have as much respect now."

"That's not true, Babu!" Shida's notebook slipped out of her hands. She fumbled to catch it. "I mean, I don't think that's true."

"Oh, I'm afraid it is, my child. When all of our cows

were let out, I tried to call the entire village of Njia Panda together to discuss what happened, but only relatives came — not even the other families who moved here with us from Litongo. People are feeling challenged by the move. They still have their pride in Nyerere and his vision, but I can see that they feel cramped in their homes and frightened by the idea of shared farming.

"And these many days when I've been working in the collective cotton fields, I've been trying to encourage Gervas's father to come work with us. Everyone in the village will share in the profits from this collective field, but only some of us come to work. I'm learning that people like Gervas's father do not share our vision — they can only think of themselves. I fear that some of our people will forget their pride in this new village and will become too self-focused, like him."

Babu shook his head. "Perhaps I'm saying too much for your young ears. In the end, I believe this move was a good decision. After the harvest of this first cotton crop, we may have enough money to buy a village tractor, and perhaps that will convince the others that shared farming is important. In the end, we'll all learn to live together."

Shida studied Babu's face. For a moment, she thought she saw a twinkle of true hope in his eyes, but then the last sliver of sun dipped below the horizon, and his face fell into shadow.

Chapter 11

When elephants fight, the grass gets hurt.
— *Tanzanian proverb*

"Grace, catch!" Shida tossed a thin, round aluminum pot toward her cousin. Grace was squatting on the other side of Mama's dirty dishes in the yard. She lifted her hands just in time for the pot to slip right through them and collide with her chest.

Grace glared at her cousin. She pulled the blouse of her dress away from her chest so she could inspect a small soot stain. "Shida, look what you've done. Why do you have to joke around all the time? This is the only dress I've got."

"Your only dress? What happened to your purple one?" Shida leapt over Mama's two other pots and rubbed water into the spot on Grace's dress. The stain faded away into a smear of water no bigger than Shida's hand.

"I looked everywhere for it this morning, but it's gone," Grace said.

"Strange," Shida said. "How come everyone's missing clothes?"

"Shhh." Grace scrubbed her pot with newfound intensity.

Shida glanced over her shoulder and froze. Mama Malongo limped along the road, carrying an enormous bundle of dried-reed brooms.

"Oh, no," Shida said.

Mama Malongo stumbled up to them. She glared at Shida with one eye. The other eye was covered in a ragged, gray headscarf, which had fallen down from under her bundle. "Lazing around as usual, I see. Better that than going to school, I suppose. The ancestors don't like girls going to school."

Shida picked up a pot — it was clean, but she scrubbed it with sand anyway. Better to keep busy than to respond to the old woman.

"The ancestors don't like girls going to school, so they've cursed this village. First your precious cow disappears, and now the village cotton crop is ruined."

Shida focused on the sound of sand on metal. The old woman was crazy. There was no point in listening to her.

But Grace's head popped up. "Which cotton crop,

Mama Malongo?"

Shida glared at Grace. What was she doing talking to Mama Malongo?

"The ancestors have cursed your Babu's special cotton crop. It's gone. Dead."

Babu's special cotton crop? Shida squinted at Mama Malongo. "What are you talking about?" she asked sharply.

Mama Malongo tilted her torso forward and let her bundle of brooms fall to the ground. "I'm talking about the collective cotton crops. They've been destroyed. Everyone's gone to see them, but I suppose you weren't around to hear the commotion. You were in school."

Shida jumped to her feet. So that's why the village was so quiet this afternoon. That's why even Mama was out.

Grace grabbed Shida's hand. "Let's go." They took off in a run.

"Beware," Mama Malongo yelled after them. "The ancestors have cursed us, and you can be sure it's because girls like you are in school . . ."

Grace and Shida sprinted down the hill that led to the school, past the clinic, and along roads lined with houses in Old Njia Panda. Grace led the way and, though Shida's legs and lungs burned with each pounding step, she kept forcing herself forward, racing toward Babu.

Shida's thoughts ran in circles ahead of her. Mama Malongo had to be confused. She was probably just lying.

All of the collective cotton gone? That was impossible. Babu had just spent a week working on those fields. He would have said something if he had seen signs of crop failure. They couldn't just be gone. If the crops were gone, then Babu would lose hope. If Babu lost hope, then Shida and her people would end up returning to Litongo, and then what?

After at least a half hour of running, first through Old Njia Panda and then through private fields, the girls spotted an enormous field, lined with rows of cotton plants. The specks of people on the periphery of the field grew larger, and Shida began to recognize some of her neighbors.

"Babu?" Shida huffed.

"He's over there." Grace pointed with a limp arm as she crouched to catch her breath.

Babu stood about three rows into the cotton field. He looked exhausted, leaning heavily on his stick. His head swiveled on his neck as he surveyed the scene. Shida scanned the field with him — rows upon rows of cotton stretched out to the horizon.

"It's amazing," Shida said.

Grace looked up. "It's dead."

Shida walked up to a nearby plant and pulled off one of its withered leaves. The tissue was scarred and brown and the stems and leaves hung down as if they had suffered through a very long drought, though this had happened overnight. Shida shivered. "What could have done this?"

A voice from just inside the first line of cotton boomed over Shida's. "The best we can do now is pull up the plants. Let's get started. We might be able to get the first section of this field before the sun goes down."

Shida stared at her uncle. Poor Uncle Bujiko. Sure he could be unreasonable, especially about sending Grace and Furaha to school, but everyone knew he'd worked hard on the collective fields. Next to him stood Mama Grace, who had quietly prayed for this move so her daughters could go to school. And around them were most of the villagers from Litongo. All of them leaned over to begin tearing their hard work out of the earth.

"Cousin Shida?"

Shida looked down to see Furaha.

"What happened, Shida? Did a person do this, Grace?"

"We don't know," Shida said.

"You think it's the witch, Mama Malongo?" Furaha's big brown eyes stared up at Shida.

"It might be Mama Malongo," Shida said, "but Babu doesn't think so."

"What about Gervas?" Grace said. She nodded in the direction of a trail that led to the field.

Gervas was lumbering toward them. At a distance, he almost looked handsome with his round body, but as he got closer, Shida could make out his sneer and his angry, squinty eyes.

Shida groaned and the two girls turned to face the cotton fields. Grace grabbed Furaha by the shoulders and turned her as well, but Gervas walked right up to them.

"*Hehehe.*" Gervas's laugh reverberated through his broad chest, like an offbeat drum. "I see your Babu's cotton crop is dead. Some say the ancestors are unhappy with him for invading our village. But then others say your clan's been cursed for sending its girls to school."

Shida clenched her fists. How dare he tease them about this crop that meant so much to Babu? How dare he joke when his family hadn't contributed a thing?

"Some say . . ." Grace turned around. "Some say, Gervas, that a witch put a curse on this crop. I happen to know this witch quite well and I can confirm that she did it."

"Witches or ancestors, either way it's a curse," Gervas said.

"Yes, but this witch isn't done," Grace said. "This witch is angry about everything. She's angry with the villagers of Litongo for moving here, especially at our Babu for leading the decision, but she's also angry with the family of Njia Panda's old chief for letting those from Litongo in. She told me the other day that she plans to put her next curse on that family. She wanted to know who the old chief is. She asked me."

Shida's mouth twitched into a grin. She squatted down,

pretending to focus on uprooting the plant in front of her.

"I told her, this witch," Grace said, "that I didn't know the old chief, but that I knew his son. I told her to go after the fat boy."

Shida forced the smile off her face and peeked at Gervas.

His eyes widened and darted around the field.

"Would you like me to introduce you to her?" Grace said. "She's not far away. In fact, I'm not sure she really needs an introduction. You do stand out."

"You're lying," Gervas said. He took two heavy steps toward Grace, already puffing. "You're lying. I know you are. I know a witch didn't do this."

"And how do you know, Gervas?" Grace said.

Gervas squinted back at her. His upper lip turned up in a sneer. "Stupid girl!" He spun around and lumbered back up the trail.

"I think we may have just heard a confession," Grace said. "How does he know a witch didn't do it? Maybe he did it himself."

"Gervas isn't smart enough to pull off something like this," Shida said. "But he did come to school late today, late enough that he could have finished whatever needed to be done to kill the crops," Grace said.

Furaha looked up. "Gervas was really late to school. He came with my teacher. Teacher Karakola was late, too. We had fun this morning. We used Kwira's *kitenge* cloth and tied each other onto our backs like we were carrying babies. And then — "

"So, Teacher Karakola came late with Gervas?" Shida said.

"Oh, yes, he must have been busy early this morning, because he was yawning all day."

The two older girls looked at each other.

"Let's meet tomorrow morning two hours before sun-up." Shida winked at Grace. "I have some extra chores to do and I'll need your help."

"Yes, I think that would be good. I'll come to your house."

And the two older girls led the chattering Furaha out into the fields, where they joined the other villagers from Litongo in pulling up the withered cotton plants, one by one.

Chapter 12

Hope is the pillar of the world.
— *Nigerian proverb*

When Shida returned home that evening, one of her young cousins was herding Babu's cattle into the corral. Shida hurried past the boy and around the corral toward Babu's cooking hut. As she approached the door, Shida thought she heard a voice in the compound. She looked over her shoulder and glimpsed red. It was Mama. She was leaning up against the thorny cattle corral.

"Mama, be careful. You'll poke yourself on the brambles." Shida strode toward her mother, ready to pull her up.

"The sun knows, Shida," Mama said.

Shida stopped. "What, Mama?" She didn't have time for this — she had to cook for Babu tonight and it was already late.

"The sun isn't stupid, Shida. It knows." Mama's gaze was tilted up to the hills where the sun was setting toward Litongo. A crow landed on the brambles behind her. It bobbed its head three times and then flew off, cawing.

"Every night the sun sinks down over those hills toward Litongo to go to sleep," Mama said. "The sun always returns home. It knows where home is. Home is Litongo, Shida."

"Mama, how do you know home isn't here in Njia Panda?" Shida said. "When we lived in Litongo, the sun began its day here. Perhaps this is where we're supposed to start over."

Mama shivered. "No, Shida. You don't understand. What's important isn't where you start over, but where you go home. I went to your father's place. Everything was supposed to be perfect. But . . . but in the end, my new beginning didn't last long. My sun set back in Litongo." Mama sniffled and rubbed her hand across her nose. A string of shiny mucus stuck to her cheek. "Home is where your sun sets, Shida. Remember that."

That night, Shida had to feed Mama. She crouched inside their hut and coaxed Mama to eat just a few bites of sweet potato. When Mama had finally taken her last bite and rolled over on her reed mat, Shida heard voices outside. She leaned out the door and saw Babu slumping toward his hut in the moonlight, braced by two companions.

"Get some rest, my father," Uncle Bujiko said.

"Yes, I will, my son." Babu settled into the cowhide chair outside his hut and looked up at Uncle Bujiko. "You've done good work today and you also worked very hard on those fields. I'm sorry to see your work lost."

"We're all sorry." Uncle Bujiko held Babu's hand for a moment, then released it. "I'm going now, Father."

"Go in peace, my son."

The other man, the younger of the two medicine men from Litongo, crouched in front of Babu's chair. "I must go, too, Grandfather. But, please, remember to do what I told you. Make the shrine."

As the medicine man walked out of the yard, Shida ran to her grandfather. "Babu, what is your news? Can I bring you dinner?"

The old man raised his head from where it had been resting on his chest. He smiled at Shida. "Yes, my daughter. I'd like my dinner, but after that I wonder if you could help me?"

"Yes, Babu." Shida would do anything, anything to ease the despair she saw weighing down her grandfather.

"The young medicine man has said that our cotton was destroyed because the ancestors are unhappy. He thinks that my father's spirit is troubled by all of this movement we've made in the last year. My father's spirit is restless."

Shida slipped into the chair next to Babu. Did this

mean they'd have to return to Litongo? Certainly life was better for Shida in Njia Panda with school and the nurse, but maybe she was being selfish. Maybe if they just went back to Litongo and Shida got married and tried to act like the young woman people were telling her to be, life would be better for Mama and Babu.

"So, my child . . ." Babu interrupted Shida's thoughts. "The medicine man has suggested that I build a spirit house for my father, your great-grandfather. This will give him a place to settle and to feel at home here in Njia Panda. I've thought about where to place this spirit house, and perhaps my father's spirit would be happiest on top of your rock."

"My rock?" Shida felt a flutter of hope in her chest — so they'd stay here, at least for now.

Babu turned his head slowly and then shifted his stiff body to look back at the kopje that loomed over the metal roof of Shida's hut. "Your rock," he said. "I'm hoping you can go up on your rock with some small pieces of wood and some grass clippings. You can make a miniature house for my father's spirit and any other spirits that feel unsettled here."

Shida looked back at Babu. One of his eyebrows twitched. He had a distracted, troubled look on his face, as if he were talking with someone else in his mind.

"Are you alright, Babu?" Shida squatted down in front of him to look into his exhausted eyes.

Babu nodded. "Yes, yes, I'm fine, simply worried. Without our cotton, we only have the tomatoes and the next sweet potato harvest to rely on. If those don't work . . ."

"Yes, Babu, if those crops don't work . . . ?"

"If those crops fail, then we'll be in real trouble. I'm beginning to think . . ." Babu's lips continued to move, as if he were speaking, but no words came.

"You're beginning to think, Babu . . ." Shida put her hands on Babu's legs, forcing herself to keep looking into his pained face.

"I'm beginning to think we might need to return to Litongo."

<hr>

After Babu had eaten that night, Shida scurried up the side of her kopje and walked out to its front. Off to one side of Njia Panda, Mama Grace's metal roof glinted in the moonlight. Grace and Furaha and Mama Grace felt close, as if their sleeping mats had been pulled right up next to Shida. The roofs of the clinic and the school stretched out in the other direction. Seeing things from up above eased some of the tension Shida had been feeling. Sure, her people would have to face challenges in this new place — perhaps even more than failed crops — but ultimately wouldn't their lives improve? "Njia Panda." Shida whispered the name of the village in front of her. Its meaning seemed fitting, and full of hope: "place where the road rises."

Shida looked down at the scraps of wood and grass she had tied into the skirt of her dress. A spirit house for her great-grandfather. She wedged two slivers of wood into notches in the granite and then added more wood, all about the height of her own hand, until she had a circle that leaned together in a point at the top.

"Great-Grandfather, I'll leave the front of your house open so you can look out over your new village."

Shida leaned out over the tiny house and peeked into the small door. She placed grass clippings inside and then fell back on her knees. The house cast a long, moonlit shadow across the rock face.

"Will you be happy here?" Shida said. She was speaking to her great-grandfather's spirit, but Shida realized with the ache she felt in her chest that really she was speaking to Babu. If living here was too much for Babu, then she was ready to go back to Litongo.

A warm gust of wind washed over Shida. The fan palm across the road rustled. The rustling turned into a continuous lapping sound, like water on a shore. The sound was like the river in Litongo, or like the sound of water in her Sukuma rock pyramid dream. Shida didn't know what the sound meant, but she closed her eyes and let the lapping flood her ears, melting some of her tension away.

"Please make this your home, Great-Grandfather. Please settle here."

Chapter 13

Supposing doesn't fill the grain basket.
— *Namibian proverb*

"Father was up even before I was this morning." Grace huffed as she strode up the hill toward the school.

Everything around them was pitch black. Shida had to squint to see her cousin. "What could he possibly be doing so early in the morning? Or is it even morning?" Shida looked up at the dark sky. The moon had set.

"He was arguing with Mama Kulwa again," Grace said. "She wanted something."

"What?" Shida swatted at a mosquito buzzing around her head.

"I don't know, but can you imagine begging for things in the middle of the night? Maybe that's why he's getting up so early every morning to work in the fields. She's probably pressuring him to come up with more money."

The two girls crested the hill that looked down toward the center of the village.

"So, Gervas's house is right about —" Grace raised her hand to point toward the dark void of Old Njia Panda, but the two girls' eyes jumped to a bright light glaring up from the school compound. It was next to Teacher Karakola's house.

Grace and Shida ran down the sandy hill to the school. They darted under the sleepy branches of the flamboyant tree and stopped by the side of the schoolroom to catch their breath. Shida peeked around the corner and signaled for Grace to follow. The bright rays of a lantern shone through holes in Teacher Karakola's corral. The two girls wove their way around the tentacles of light and up to the edge of the corral. They climbed up on the brambles to peek over at the teacher's house. The lantern sat outside the corrugated metal door.

"He's really crazy," Shida said. "Who would ever turn a lantern up that high? No one can afford kerosene like that."

Grace shoved her hand over Shida's mouth. From around one corner of the house, the figure of Teacher Karakola strode toward the lantern. He wore a light blue shirt and white dress pants that reflected back the light in a glare. The girls ducked down behind the corral.

Teacher Karakola laughed to himself as he picked up the lantern. The spray of light approached them from around the corral. Shida stopped breathing and squeezed herself into a ball. An enormous sandal pounded down on the dirt beside her and then everything around them was flooded in a bleached glow of white. Shida shifted her weight to the balls of her feet. How had she gotten herself into this situation again? But then a veil of darkness descended back over them. Teacher Karakola had rounded the side of the schoolhouse.

"Do you think he could have killed all those cotton plants with kerosene?" Grace said.

Shida's heart was still pounding. "Kerosene?" It seemed crazy, but so did burning a lantern that brightly.

Following Teacher Karakola wasn't difficult. He was a walking ball of bright, swinging light that sent lizards and mice on the side of the road scurrying back into the cover of darkness.

"Do you think he's going to the cotton fields?" Shida said. "He's already killed everything there, hasn't he?"

Grace's head bobbed up and down. "Maybe he wants to place a curse on the field so nothing new can grow."

Whatever he was up to, they were going to catch him.

But halfway through Old Njia Panda, Teacher Karakola's light veered off the road and into a large compound.

The front door of a big house swung open and Gervas's

heavy body filled the doorframe. He stepped into the yard, followed by a tall, broad-shouldered man.

The big man greeted Teacher Karakola, though at their distance, Shida and Grace could only decipher a few words. "You and my boy . . . great things . . ."

Shida and Grace ran closer.

"Scare those girls away . . . I'll give you whatever you need — more kerosene, anything. Just come every morning and keep moving. You must stay active to get this job done."

Gervas's father turned and disappeared into the darkness of the big house. Gervas and Karakola lumbered across the dirt courtyard to the main road. The teacher shoved his palm in the middle of Gervas's thick shoulders, prodding him down the road.

Grace and Shida took off in a jog to catch up. "When they get to the fields, my father will be there," Grace said. "But if we can just get ahead of them, then we can tell Father to hide and watch what they do next."

The girls tried running around the side of the pool of light, but each time they made any progress, leaves in the ditch crackled under their feet and they ended up retreating to the middle of the road behind Gervas and the teacher.

"We'll just have to hope they don't see Uncle Bujiko," Shida said.

Teacher Karakola pushed Gervas off the main road and

onto a small path.

Grace stopped. "But this path leads back to the school, not to the fields."

"Shhh," Shida said. She grabbed Grace's hand and pulled her off the road, following the light.

A moment later, they heard Gervas's voice from the path ahead. "Why do we have to keep walking?"

"Your father insisted we keep moving, you little dog. And he's right. Unless you're moving, you get distracted and you never end up learning anything. I can't imagine what you do in Teacher Mrefu's class all day."

Gervas sneered. "I mostly poke those stupid girls with my stick."

Teacher Karakola stopped on the path.

Grace and Shida jumped back from the light.

"Well, you should be working at beating those girls in subjects, not with some stupid stick. Now, let's get back to it." Teacher Karakola began walking again. He hopped over a stream of biting *siafu* ants, but Gervas's foot brushed it.

"28 plus 20 is?" Karakola pushed Gervas ahead.

"42?"

"No, you idiot. It's 48." Teacher Karakola turned his head up to the dark sky. "Okay, if you don't know math, then how's your writing?" He careened over to the side of the road and snapped off a twig. "Here." He handed the stick to Gervas. "Write your name. You should at least be able to manage that."

Gervas fiddled with the stick.

"Come on." Teacher Karakola shoved Gervas into a squat. "Write you name in the dirt."

"I don't care about writing."

Teacher Karakola threw down his arms. "And your father expects me to teach you enough to argue that those girls are slowing down lessons? There's no way we'll get rid of them. You're hopeless!"

Teacher Karakola kicked at the dirt and then stormed down the path toward the school. Gervas stood alone, quickly fading into darkness.

"Hmmf! Who needs him anyway? I'd rather sleep than walk in circles, doing some stupid lessons."

Grace's mouth brushed up against Shida's ear. "He'll come back this way."

The two girls shimmied sideways until their feet met brittle grass. They hunched down.

"Ahhh!" Gervas suddenly shouted. The shouts grew louder and soon turned into a high-pitched screech.

"Siafu ants!" Shida's whisper shook with a giggle. Twenty *siafu* could attach themselves to a human foot if its owner had the misfortune of stepping on their trail, but the ants always took a few minutes to distribute themselves across the body before they started biting.

Footsteps thudded along the trail toward them.

Something soft brushed Shida's feet. She reached out —
cotton.

"His shirt's off, Grace. His pants are probably just up
the path."

Gervas's shouts disappeared up the trail and the two
girls clutched their stomachs, dissolving into laughter.

"Okay, it's not exactly what I'd hoped," Shida said.
"He's not getting eaten alive in a pit of *siafu* ants, but this
is pretty good."

"Good?" Grace said. "This is great!"

Chapter 14

Children are the reward of life.
— Congolese proverb

The pleasure of imagining Gervas running home naked and covered in ants wore off quickly, and Shida and Grace slumped back toward the center of the village. If Gervas and Teacher Karakola had been sabotaging the new villagers in Njia Panda, they showed no signs of guilt now. Teacher Karakola still could have poisoned the collective cotton, but he probably came late to school only because Gervas couldn't learn simple math. And Gervas? Gervas was too dumb to kill even one cotton plant.

So who could it be? Mama Malongo? Or were the ancestors unhappy with Shida's people? Shida found herself mulling over the same question all day at school, when her eyes weren't fading into sleepy oblivion as Teacher Mrefu led the class in a lesson on writing.

After classes that day, while they waited for Furaha, Grace and Shida crouched on the side of the road, trying to come up with a new plan. But when Furaha emerged from the school gate, they both stopped talking. Her head was downcast and she shuffled slowly over the sand.

"What's wrong, Furaha?" Shida said. The little girl slouched in front of them. She looked like a wet dress hanging limp on a tree after washing.

"I'm tired, Gracey. I'm going to start walking home." She turned and started up the road.

"That's not like Furaha," Shida said.

"She probably got in trouble with Teacher Karakola," Grace said. "She'll be fine."

They began to follow Furaha, but a voice stopped them.

"Shida, is that you?"

The girls turned.

"*Shikamoo*, Nurse Goldfilda," Shida said. She bent down on her knee.

Nurse Goldfilda waved her up. "You're coming to the clinic today, aren't you? Oh, I'll be so relieved to have your help, Shida. I have blood slides from three patients that I need to read for malaria, and I just had to run out to the junction to collect a delivery from Mwanza town." The nurse pointed to the box braced on her round hip. "There's so much to do."

"Yes, of course I'm coming," Shida said. Was today already Tuesday?

✗✗✗✗✗✗✗✗✗✗✗✗✗✗✗✗✗✗

When they arrived at the clinic, Nurse Goldfilda plowed up the stairs, not bothering to remove her shoes at the door. Inside the lab, she grabbed a pair of scissors and sliced through the twine lacing on the box. She flipped open the top. *"Aha!"* She stood back with her hands on her hips to admire the box's contents.

Shida rolled onto the balls of her feet so she could see better.

Nurse Goldfilda lifted a red print blouse and skirt out of the box. "Do you like them?"

"That's . . . I mean . . . they're very nice," Shida said. They were beautiful. Beautiful and way too small for the nurse.

"Well, they're for you, Shida! I hope you like them."

Shida gulped and then hiccupped. She covered her mouth.

Nurse Goldfilda started laughing, and soon Shida joined her.

"They're the most beautiful clothes I've ever seen," Shida said.

The nurse held up the skirt for Shida to admire. It was long and straight, a wrap skirt that tied at the waist, though

155

Shida could see that it had been carefully tailored to flair slightly at the hips and then again down below the knees. It wasn't heavily layered with pleats, like a little girl's dress. Instead, it reminded Shida of the skirts that stylish young women in the village had begun wearing. The material looked like it was brand new *kitenge* cloth — a red background printed with black giraffes and white birds on their backs.

"It's amazing," Shida said.

The nurse smiled and held up the blouse. It was even more beautiful. The two sides came together in an overlapping zigzag with large cloth-covered buttons and two puffy sleeves. All of the women in Njia Panda would dream of this outfit, even Mama Kulwa. But Shida?

"I, uh . . . they're too beautiful for me."

"Of course they're not. Try them on." Nurse Goldfilda handed the skirt and blouse to Shida and strode out of the room.

Shida bent down to peek under the curtain covering the doorway. The nurse's white shoes stared back at her. Shida untied her medicine pouch from her waist and pulled her filthy green dress over her head. She wrapped the long skirt around her middle and fed her arms into the blouse. The material felt rough and new, but wonderfully loose. Shida swung her arms and spread her legs, bending her knees. She inhaled a deep breath, allowing her chest to expand in a way that it hadn't in ages.

"So?" The nurse peeked around the side of the curtain. "Oh, Shida!" She strode into the room and held Shida by her shoulders. "You look beautiful!" The nurse grabbed a mirror.

Shida stepped back until she could see most of herself. She tied on her medicine pouch. The young woman who stared back at her looked confident and mature.

"I love them," Shida said. "But why me?"

"Why you? Let me count the reasons. You helped me with Baby Lewanga last week — I couldn't have done that myself. You're going to be my medical ambassador to this village. People trust you and with your help they'll trust me. You speak Swahili, so I can actually talk to you. And . . ." The nurse looked down. "And, well, you're my best hope for a friend. I mean, really, what's a single girl like me who doesn't speak Sukuma supposed to do for friends in a village like this?"

"You're not a girl," Shida sputtered. And yet the nurse was chattering away like one of Shida's girlfriends. Shida studied the nurse's face, noticing for the first time the lack of wrinkles around her eyes. "Okay, you have to be at least twenty years old, so at the very least you're not single."

The nurse laughed. "You're right about my age — I am twenty — but I'm serious, I'm not married."

Shida's jaw dropped. Not married at twenty? The

only women not married at twenty in Litongo were . . . Well, there weren't any. "How come you're not married?" Shida felt as if she were asking the nurse to reveal a terrible family curse or something.

"Well, I finished my studies just this last year and I begged my parents to let me start my career before marriage. They already felt I was too old to be unwed, even for a city girl, but I knew if I started working before they married me, then my husband would think of me as a working woman. He'd be more likely to let me keep working after I moved into his home."

Shida nodded and felt a familiar warmness flood her. It was a feeling she got when she talked with Grace, whose struggles were so similar to her own that they helped Shida understand herself. "You mean I'm not crazy to think I don't want to get married?"

Nurse Goldfilda widened her eyes and huffed. "No, what a waste." She laughed. "Well, let's just say, I don't think you're crazy. My parents would probably say you are."

"How did you convince your parents?" Shida raised an eyebrow.

"I didn't have to. President Nyerere advertised for nurses and when he offered me this job to work in one of his first *ujamaa* villages, my parents were so excited, they forgot about marriage, at least for the time being.

"Oh, you're lucky," Shida said.

Nurse Goldfilda frowned at Shida. "Well, let's make you lucky. You're already a better healer than I am in a lot of ways, and if I can teach you about my medicines, then maybe you'll be so indispensable that people will think of you as a grown-up woman and they'll just forget about Shida the girl who ought to have a husband."

Shida smiled and raised her eyebrows. "That sure would be nice."

"Okay." Nurse Goldfilda clapped her hands. "Let's get to work, then, shall we? I think I've got some chemicals in here." She reached into the box and pulled out two bottles of dark blue liquid. "Yes, this is it. We can use these to read the blood slides for malaria. Have I shown you how to do this yet?"

And soon Shida was applying drops of chemicals to stain the blood slides and taking turns peering into the microscope with the nurse, looking for the dark malarial parasites. All worries from outside the clinic walls seemed to fade away, and now Shida was twirling around the lab, a young woman working as a nurse's apprentice.

Over the next few hours, patients wandered in. Shida doled out medicine, drew blood for more tests, and helped wrap a young boy's badly swollen ankle. All of the patients commented on Shida's outfit. "You look beautiful, Miss Shida."

When Shida walked the last patient to the door, the

sun was already on a steep decline.

"I really should go, before the sun's set completely," Shida said. "I have to get home to help my mother with dinner." Shida took off the white apron the nurse had loaned her and carefully folded it in quarters before handing it back. "Thanks very much for the skirt and blouse. I love them."

"Oh, you're welcome, Shida. Thanks for the company and the help. It's nice to have a friend in Njia Panda."

Nurse Goldfilda was smiling, but Shida felt her heart sink. Yes, Njia Panda. Shida was beginning to have her doubts she'd be living in Njia Panda too much longer.

<hr>

The next morning, Shida woke to Grace standing in her doorway.

"Shida!"

Shida bolted up from her mat and rubbed her face. "Are we late for school?"

The morning sun streamed around Grace. Shida could just make out the shadowy features of her cousin's face. Grace's eyes were red and her cheeks hung with fatigue.

"Shida, it's Furaha. She's had fever all night and her legs and arms ache. The young medicine man says it's a curse."

Mama stirred on the reed mats behind them.

"Is Shida there?" A man's voice boomed in the yard.

Grace grabbed Shida's arm and pulled her out of the

hut. Shida blinked in the bright sunlight. In front of her was Uncle Bujiko, with little Furaha's limp body draped across his arms. Mama Grace hovered over her youngest daughter, and Babu leaned heavily on his walking stick with the handsome young medicine man beside him.

"We're sorry to wake you, daughter." Babu's cheek trembled slightly as he spoke. "But your cousin here is quite sick, and the medicine man tells us she's been cursed. It seems our ancestors are still angry with me."

"But I built the spirit house, Babu," Shida said.

"Yes, my daughter. You built a very nice house for my father's spirit. I could see it from the road yesterday. But early this morning, Bujiko and the medicine man carried Furaha up there to plead with my father's spirit, and the house was gone."

"What did you use to build the house?" the medicine man said. He was tall and muscular with beautiful, dark skin.

"I . . . I used bark and grass, but I wedged them into the rock. I suppose with a strong wind some of it could have fallen down, but the wood would still be there."

"There was nothing up there," Uncle Bujiko barked.

"Nothing?" Shida's eyes pinched into a squint.

"Never mind," Babu said. "They've rebuilt the house and asked my father's spirit to be kind to the girl, but in the meantime, we must take her home to care for her. We thought you might help with that, Shida."

Shida's eyes fell back on Furaha. The little girl's plump body dangled over her father's burly arms. Her mouth hung open. Shida placed her hand on the little girl's forehead. It was raging with heat.

"Yes, Babu. Of course I'll help."

<hr>

Uncle Bujiko settled Furaha into a corner of Mama Grace's hut. Grace and her mother bundled Furaha with every bit of clothing from their three-person house, but with each nudge and tuck, Furaha remained listless.

Shida knelt down next to her cousin, running her hands up and down the girl's body. Shida couldn't remember ever having felt so much heat coming off a child. Furaha had a terrible fever — that was certain.

"Has she had diarrhea?" Shida said.

"No, Shida." Mama Grace whispered over her shoulder.

"Any foul-smelling burps or gas?"

"No."

So no dysentery. Shida's class notes from Nurse Goldfilda's lecture about malaria flashed in her head. Fever and aching joints. Shida gently squeezed Furaha's knees and elbows, keeping her eyes on the little girl's face. Furaha's eyebrows squeezed together in a wince.

"Has she been complaining of pain in her elbows

and knees?"

"Yes, she kept gripping her elbows last night and whimpering." Grace squatted down to face Shida. "Can you do something for her, Shida?"

Shida rolled back on her knees and looked up at Grace. Grace looked almost hollow, like she had three years ago when the sweet potato crop failed and they went with too little to eat.

"I'm pretty sure she has malaria," Shida said.

"Malaria and a curse?" Grace's voice was pleading, as if she were begging Shida to change her mind and suggest that her little sister had a passing cold. "What are we going to do, Shida?"

Shida sprang to her feet. "I'm going to get the nurse. She'll know what to do." Shida turned toward the door, but a familiar wrinkled hand grabbed her forearm.

"Shida, the young medicine man here says Furaha has been cursed." Babu spoke so quickly, Shida almost didn't recognize him. "My father's spirit is unhappy and we must bring him peace in order to heal the girl. We're going right now to offer a goat as sacrifice, but I hate to leave Furaha. Please stay here to take care of her while I'm gone."

Shida looked at her feet. She could give Furaha her *mamihigo* bark steam treatment, but something told her the nurse's medicine would work better. "Babu, I think Furaha has a sickness called malaria that the nurse can treat. If I'm right, the nurse will give her quinine pills that will kill the parasites in her blood."

"Oh, dear Shida." Babu's upper lip quivered and his eyes filled with tears. "I wish this were a sickness the nurse could cure, but I'm certain it's a curse this time. The nurse is a good woman and I trust her medicine, but as you know, her pills will not reverse a curse."

Shida nodded at the floor. Of course Babu was right. Some sicknesses were caused by curses or unhappy spirits, and the nurse's white pills certainly couldn't cure Furaha of that.

"Well, then, at least let me treat Furaha with *mamihigo* steam," Shida said. "It'll calm her and it might even drive her fever down." Shida watched her little cousin's chest rise and fall with labored breaths.

"Yes, Shida, please do that." Babu clasped Shida's hand. "Your medicine is familiar even to my father's spirit, and I'll feel better knowing you're taking care of little Furaha while I'm gone."

Babu turned to the young *mganga* who had been waiting next to him. "Let's go get the goat."

⚹⚹⚹⚹⚹⚹⚹⚹⚹⚹⚹⚹⚹⚹⚹

Shida sent a child to collect two handfuls of bark from a tree just up the road. Meanwhile, she told Uncle Bujiko's youngest wife to gather as many red coals as she could find and to set a large pot to boil. When her ingredients were ready, Shida boiled the *mamihigo* tree bark on a fire outside until it sent up a pungent steam. She carried the big pot inside, and eased it down next to the mats where Furaha rested.

"I need a strong *kitenge* cloth with no holes in it," Shida said.

Mama Grace unraveled her head wrap. It was tattered.

Shida marched out of the hut and right up to Uncle Bujiko. "Please, Uncle, I need one of Mama Kulwa's *kitenge* cloth. They're the only *kitenge* around here with no holes."

In a few minutes, Uncle Bujiko ducked into Mama Grace's hut holding one of Mama Kulwa's wrap skirts.

Shida sat down on the mats where Furaha was resting and swung one leg behind her tiny cousin. Bracing Furaha's floppy head, Shida propped the little girl up against her own chest and then rotated on the mat so their feet encircled the hot pot.

"Cover us with the cloth, Grace," Shida said.

Grace billowed the *kitenge* cloth over their heads and the pot, sealing it shut on one side as Mama Grace held it down on the other. Soon, Shida could feel the hot steam filling the trapped air around them.

"Breathe in, breathe in, little cousin," Shida said. "You remember how you always wanted me to call you Baraka? You always wanted to be my patient with good fortune. Well, when you were a baby and sick, I wasn't a healer yet, but now is our time, Baraka."

Furaha shivered in Shida's lap.

"That's right. Good, Baraka. Breathe the steam in deeply."

Shida felt Furaha's chest rise and fall. The steam billowed up around them, filling their little cloth tent.

Shida lifted her hands to Furaha's head of damp, tightly curled hair. "Little Furaha, you know what your name means," Shida whispered in her ear. "Happiness, yes? You're your mother's happiness, Furaha, and your sister's happiness, and your Babu's happiness, and even your father's happiness. You're my happiness. You know that children are the most valuable thing a Sukuma can have, more valuable than cotton crops or even cows. We need you to get better and stay with us, Furaha."

Under Shida's trembling hands, Furaha's whole body rose with another deep breath.

Chapter 15

Unless you call out, who will open the door?
— *Ethiopian proverb*

By evening, Shida had finished three rounds of steam treatment with Furaha. The little girl's breathing was steadier now, and she was shivering. Shida hoped the shivering would drive out the bad spirit or sickness. But Furaha's tiny body was still raging with heat and the few times she spoke, she moaned about pain in her legs and arms.

Babu entered the hut and lowered himself down on his knees next to Shida. His breath was quick and labored, and Shida wondered how far they had gone for the goat sacrifice. "How is the little one?" In the contrasting glow of warm lantern light, his face was carved with thick curves of worry.

"She's a little bit better, Babu, but she has all the symptoms of malaria. The *mamihigo* steam is helping her, but I still think we should call the nurse."

"Oh, dear child, I'm certain the ancestors or someone in this village is angry with me. They're punishing me through this innocent girl. But now that I'm back and can be with Furaha, you certainly can go get the nurse. I don't believe her medicine will help us, but she's welcome here, of course. Just promise me one thing." Babu placed a hand on Shida's shoulder. "Go protect the spirit house on your kopje tonight. Make sure it doesn't come to any harm."

"I'll do both, Babu."

Shida turned and stretched her arms across the backs of Mama Grace and Grace.

Grace grabbed one of Shida's hands and Mama Grace turned to Shida. "Please, Shida, do anything you can. I thought we'd lose Furaha when she was a baby and her food and water ran right through her, but she's been so well these last few years. I can't lose her now."

Shida nodded and looked into her aunt's eyes. "I'll do everything I can."

Shida didn't allow herself a moment more to think. She ducked out of the hut's low door and strode through the small crowd of adults lingering outside the house. And then Shida ran, all the way to the clinic. She sailed through the door and across the waiting room, pushing the curtain aside.

Nurse Goldfilda jerked her head up from a stack of papers. "Oh, Shida, you scared me. What's wrong?"

"It's my little cousin, Furaha. The one who's always laughing and dancing. I think it's malaria."

The nurse stood up and grabbed her black bag from the countertop. She blew out her lantern. "Shida, there's no way she can come here for a blood test, is there?" The nurse was already walking out of the lab.

Shida followed her. "No, she's very sick."

"But you're sure of the symptoms? Then let's give her quinine right away."

✗✗✗✗✗✗✗✗✗✗✗✗✗✗✗

When they reached Babu's compound, Shida stayed behind while the nurse hurried up the road. Though Shida was certain Furaha should take medicine for malaria, she was equally certain she should guard the spirit house that night. Parasites were responsible for some sicknesses and curses for others, and in this case, they needed to protect against both.

Shida stood next to the cattle corral, staring up at the top of her kopje. The moon had risen and Shida could just make out the dainty lines of the spirit house at the edge of the granite precipice.

"I hear Bujiko's little girl is cursed." A hoarse voice drifted toward Shida on the warm night air.

"Mama?" Shida said.

"Poor child. It's not her fault. I suppose it's never that way, though. Curses are never fair. Whatever it was that killed your father, he certainly never deserved to die."

"You think Father was cursed?" Shida walked over to her mother and crouched down next to her in the dirt.

"Oh, who knows? Most of the villagers of Litongo seem to think I cursed him. His mother certainly believed I did. But if anyone cursed him, she did. His mother was angry to see her son shifting his loyalties from her to me."

Shida's eyes widened.

"It seemed like she was planning something right before your birth. Maybe she thought she could curse me to be rid of us. If she did curse us, it backfired. For a long time, I blamed myself for your father's death, but now I believe she cursed him. Your grandmother killed her own son."

Shida held her breath.

Mama shifted against the wall and turned her head to look up at the moon. Two eyes, rimmed in white, glistened in the darkness. "Have you tried to heal the child, Shida?"

"Yes," Shida said.

"Did you use *mamihigo* steam? I hear the girl has a fever. *Mamihigo* steam is best for that."

Shida stared at her mother. "Yes, I did, Mama, but she's still very sick."

"I don't suppose you'll be sleeping here. I suppose you'll

be out trying to save the little girl. You always are. It seems funny to have a cursed girl trying to save another, but perhaps there's something to that." Mama turned to Shida. "Where will you sleep?"

"On top of the kopje." Shida's lips moved, but her eyes stayed locked on Mama.

"Next to the spirit house? I thought you might." Mama raised one of her arms. It was draped in something. "Here, take my *kitenge* cloth to cover yourself. The mosquitoes will be bad."

Shida looked at the cloth her mother held out to her. How had Mama known?

"Take it," Mama said.

On top of the kopje, Shida curled up in a ball next to the small spirit house. Mosquitoes flitted through the humid air like minnows in a lake, but Shida covered herself entirely with Mama's *kitenge* cloth, all of herself except one eye. With that eye, Shida peeked out through a tattered hole at the spirit house and beyond it to Mama Grace's house, where Furaha was being treated for malaria.

Thoughts began to blur and Shida felt herself sinking into sleep. Soon the spirit house blended into the Sukuma rock pyramid and Shida was on the lowest ring of a stack of granite kopjes piled up toward the sky. She wore a dress of *mamihigo* bark dyed in red, and on each of the enormous kopjes above played a child. Shida looked up at the nearest kopje and there was Furaha, dancing.

"Come dance with me, Cousin Shida. I can climb on your back and then we'll be as tall as two people dancing." Furaha was wearing Shida's lost yellow dress. It was baggy around her tiny waist and shoulders.

"You look good in your new dress, Furaha."

Furaha twirled on her kopje stage and then stumbled. Shida jumped back on her rock and threw out her arms, ready to catch the little girl, but Furaha regained her balance. She swayed on her two little feet. "Come dance with me, Shida. *Pleeease.*"

"I'll come dance later, Furaha. But right now I have to stay down here. I have to keep circling our pyramid to keep an eye on all of you. I'm here to protect you so none of you fall."

Furaha stuck out her lip in a pout, but she seemed to understand. Soon, she was stomping her feet and leaping in circles once again.

Shida watched for a moment. The little girl had rhythm. Shida almost felt the rhythm in her own body. And then something cool licked her heel. Shida looked down to watch a wave splash her feet.

It was the waves. Furaha was dancing to the rhythm of the waves.

Chapter 16

To be without a friend is to be poor indeed.
— *Tanzanian proverb*

"Shida! Shida, wake up!"

Shida jumped up from the rock, tripping on Mama's *kitenge* cloth and nearly knocking over the spirit house. It stood upright, peaceful and untouched.

"Shida, listen." Mama's voice rose from the ground below.

A rooster crowed and then Shida heard it — a faint, high-pitched sound coming from the direction of the pump.

"Wailing, Shida," Mama said.

Shida's eyes darted toward Mama Grace's hut. Four people stood in the yard, but more were approaching on the road as the sun breached the horizon. Shida's chest sank and then her insides heaved up against her ribs.

"Not Furaha." Shida pleaded to the ancestors as she slid off the kopje on her stomach.

Mama stood in front of her. Her eyes were bloodshot and her face was droopy with fatigue. "Go and check on the girl, Shida."

"I will, Mama."

Shida's feet were moving and she was passing the water pump before she even realized she was running. "Come on, Furaha. Come on, little girl. Be with us. Be with us."

A small circle of women wailed in Uncle Bujiko's yard. Shida stumbled into their sea of bright orange and blue and red *kitenge*.

"Why, oh why did the little one have to go?" one voice moaned.

"Why the little happy one? She was not ready."

Shida crouched down, holding her head, trying to keep out the blue and orange and red, trying to keep out the voices. They were suffocating her, stealing the breath from her.

Hands grabbed Shida under the arms and pulled her up. "Young Shida."

Shida opened her eyes — the colors were still swimming with the voices.

"Shida!" One voice was strong.

Shida tried to focus on the voice in front of her. A flash of white. A face. The nurse came into focus.

"Shida, I'm so sorry. I tried. She was getting better through the night, but a few hours ago, the fever took over her body, and then . . ." The nurse bit her lip. "I should have called you, Shida, but I wasn't thinking there at the end." She took a deep breath. "Shida, your cousin Grace needs you now."

Grace. The name echoed in Shida's head. It echoed in a great emptiness; it echoed alone.

"Shida, look at me!"

Shida focused on the nurse's eyes.

"Grace needs you, Shida. This is part of healing, too. Go in there and help her, Shida."

Shida stumbled toward Mama Grace's hut and ducked inside. Mama Grace and Grace were right where Shida had left them, hunched over little Furaha, only now the little girl's body was enshrouded in a *kitenge* cloth. Grief and death dripped from every corner of the room.

Shida collapsed onto Grace's stiff torso. Mama Grace's quiet weeping filled the room, but then Grace convulsed. A deep, sad moan came out of her body. The moan was long and slow, like the call of a lone wildebeest, abandoned by its herd to die in the Serengeti.

Mama Grace pulled the two girls into a hug. Shida felt a hand on her shoulder and she turned to see Babu. The wrinkles under his eyes were puffy and wet.

"Shida, will you go get the girl's father?" Babu's voice cracked. "Bujiko went to work on my fields in the night. You know how he is. He can't let himself feel, and so he works. Please go, Shida. He doesn't know."

Shida nodded and then turned to the enshrouded body on the floor. She placed her hand on the rise of cloth where Furaha's feet poked up. The little girl's toes were still slightly warm.

Dead.

Dead.

Those little toes.

Shida's chest convulsed, but she stumbled to her feet and ducked through the door. She crossed the road and ran along a path that veered out around Mama Malongo's compound to Babu's fields. When she reached the edge of Babu's maize plot, Shida spotted Uncle Bujiko in a sea of knee-deep plants. He was shaking his hands over the maize, probably fertilizing it with the powder Teacher Mrefu had been teaching adults to use on the collective farms.

Shida wiped the back of her arm across her face, smearing dirt and tears together.

Uncle Bujiko looked up and jerked his hands down by his sides. "Shida, what are you doing here?" He strode toward her, the muscles in his arms and face twitching.

Shida stepped back. "I, uh . . . ." Mucus bubbled out of

her nose.

"What could you possibly want at this hour?"

"Furaha's dead."

Uncle Bujiko reached out to brace himself. "She's . . . she's dead? But . . . That can't be possible. I . . . I should have . . ." He was staring straight into the morning sun.

"You should have what, Uncle? There's nothing you could have done."

But Uncle Bujiko was running across the field toward his compound, stretching his enormous arms and legs longer and longer with each stride as if speed could bring Furaha back.

There was nothing he could have done. Nothing could have been done, other than . . . Shida watched Uncle Bujiko disappear behind a tree. Other than calling the nurse to come earlier.

The nurse's little white pills.

The pills never failed.

They had to be given soon enough, but otherwise, they never failed.

"I should have called the nurse sooner." Shida dropped to her knees in the middle of a row of corn. "Furaha had malaria. If I'd called the nurse sooner, Furaha would be here. Furaha wouldn't be dead."

<hr>

When she returned to the compound, Shida averted her

eyes as she slipped past Mama Grace, who was sitting at the door of her hut, greeting a stream of mourners. Shida knelt next to Grace, but didn't say anything. How could she? How did she even have the right to be here? She had known from the moment she saw Furaha yesterday morning that she should call the nurse. Furaha's legs and arms had been aching. Of course it had been malaria. The nurse's pills always cured malaria. Babu had been right about the cotton disaster being a curse, but Furaha's sickness was different. Why had Shida waited to call the nurse only after it was too late?

Grace reached under the shroud and pulled out one of Furaha's limp hands. The skin looked dusty and dry with a tiny web of white, cracked lines. She turned to Shida.

"We need to clean her?" Shida gulped. So this would be the beginning of her punishment, uncovering and washing Furaha's dead body, inspecting every little bit of her dear cousin, every bit she had failed to save.

Shida called one of her young cousins who was hovering outside the hut, and told her to bring a pot of warm water. When the water arrived, Shida removed the shroud.

Here was Furaha, the same little girl with her striped dress and her round belly, but that was all, only the body. Furaha's smile was gone. All of her questions and fidgeting were gone, and her eyes, her eyes were cold and glossy.

Shida squeezed a cloth in the water bowl and willed her

hand towards Furaha's hair. Funeral drums outside started beating. Shida rubbed water into the little girl's tight, oily curls and then dried them with a second cloth.

"Why, why didn't you go to the nurse sooner?" said the hair.

Shida gulped and forced her hand down to Furaha's cheeks. She flinched. The flesh was cool and limp.

"Why, why didn't you save us?" asked the cheeks.

Tears streamed down Shida's face, but she kept cleaning Furaha's body, stroking each arm and leg and hand she had failed to save.

Chapter 17

No matter how long the night, the day is sure to come.
— *Congolese proverb*

For the rest of that day and through the next, the entire village of Njia Panda seemed to flow onto the compound. Men crouched in one corner of the yard, talking softly, making plans for the coffin and burial, collecting money and food contributions from the mourners, and playing *bao* with black stones on a wooden board. The other half of the yard was a sea of women in bright *kitenge* cloth. Some women sang and tossed rice in flat baskets to sort out tiny pebbles before it was cooked. Others made flower wreaths with bright purple and pink bougainvillea blossoms and cooked large vats of food over wood fires. At night, the mourners crouched under *kitenge* cloths in the yard and tried to sleep. Other than the activity in Uncle Bujiko's yard, everything stopped. No farming, no school. Two days for Furaha.

Furaha. The little girl's name rang in Shida's head as she crouched next to Grace, silently begging the forgiveness of everyone there. Every few hours, Shida pulled herself together, answering for Grace, who refused to speak. But in between, Shida found herself running to the back of the compound to gag behind an acacia tree. How had she ever called herself a healer? All of the broken bones, fevers, and congested breathing Shida had healed paled in comparison to her failure with Furaha.

On the second afternoon, when it seemed as if all of Njia Panda were there, four of Shida's uncles carried Furaha's body out into the yard in a small wooden coffin. The men settled the coffin on two wooden braces. The top portion was still open, leaving just enough space for people to see the little girl's face.

One of Shida's aunts approached the coffin to remove the white shroud. There was silence for a moment. Then a group of women started up a song in Sukuma:

Yoooou, you left us alone,
Who will we stay with?
What will we do?
There is no one to help us.
We've come to the end.

Shida stood next to Grace, trying to block out the song. How could they blame Furaha? How could they say she didn't want to help them? Didn't they know Furaha hadn't wanted to leave?

Singing spread through the yard until a whole village of voices reverberated out of the compound. Shida watched each mourner step up to the coffin, peek over the edge to say goodbye to little Furaha, and slump away, struggling to keep up with the song. Mama Nganza was followed by Teacher Mrefu, and then Teacher Karakola strode up, followed by Gervas and his father. Shida felt nothing at the sight of her old enemies. The guilt pounding inside of her head with each mourner's step and breath of song had taken over.

Shida felt a tug at her hand. It was Grace. Grace pulled them across the yard, until hands pushed them forward, up to the coffin. Grace leaned over the wooden edge.

"Goodbye, baby sister. You'll always be my happiness. Always." Grace's tears poured onto Furaha's stony face.

Shida stared at the edge of the coffin. And then hands pushed them away. Away. The sound of her own feet pounding away from Furaha filled Shida's head. She hadn't pleaded for Furaha's forgiveness.

She hadn't even said goodbye.

After Uncle Bujiko and Mama Grace said their good-byes, the coffin was nailed shut and carried to the edge of

Uncle Bujiko's fields, where Furaha was buried under the branches of a flamboyant tree.

As the last of the mourners headed back toward the village and Mama Grace led Grace back to their hut, Shida stared up at the huge red canopy hanging over Furaha's grave. Shida had lied to Furaha about flamboyant flowers, that if one fell on a girl's head she'd be beautiful forever.

Shida picked up a red blossom and tore it to pieces. She snatched up more blossoms and flung them down at the ugly earth that held her cousin.

"Ahhh!" Shida's scream pierced the dense branches overhead and stabbed into the sky. "How could I do this! How could I ever call myself a healer?"

Her hands fumbled with the familiar knot of leather string that held her medicine pouch around her waist. Shida jerked it off and spun around in a circle until her hand let go of the leather and sent it flying, out over Furaha's grave, out toward the hills that led to Litongo.

"Never again. I'll never pretend to heal anyone again."

The pouch landed not too far away, not even outside the circle of fallen flamboyant flowers.

Shida sunk to the ground, sobbing.

A monkey shook the canopy of flowers overhead.

"You can't do that, Shida." Hands fell on Shida's back, causing her to jump. "Don't lose yourself, like I did."

Shida turned to see Mama crouching behind her. Just

over Mama's shoulder was the nurse.

"Shida," the nurse said. She fell down on her knees next to Mama. Tears were running down her face. "What makes you think you're responsible for any of this? How can you say you'll never heal again? You came to get me. You treated Furaha with *mamihigo* steam."

"I didn't come to get you soon enough." Shida sputtered for breath. "I guessed she had malaria that very first morning. If I had come in time, you would have been able to give her at least one more dose of quinine. It would have cured her. I don't know what I was thinking. Your magical pills always work."

"Shida!" The nurse gripped Shida's shoulders. "Shida, listen to me. My pills aren't magic. Do you understand? They don't always work. I've had lots of patients die. I'm pretty sure Furaha had malaria, but she had a very bad case. I think it was cerebral malaria. That's the worst kind. My pills don't stand much of a chance against it, especially not with small children. Twelve hours wouldn't have made much of a difference. You have to understand that. Even if you'd come earlier, I probably couldn't have saved her."

But all Shida could hear was the "probably" in the nurse's words.

"Shida! Shida!" Mama was shaking her now.

Shida's head snapped back and forth. The shaking felt good.

"Shida! Don't you dare give up like this. Open your eyes and look at me. Open them!"

Mama's face rippled in front of Shida.

"I told you the story about your birth before we left Litongo. I told you about the young woman Albina who had the baby, Shida, and whose husband, Milembe, died. I told you about how Milembe's mother said Albina and the baby Shida had cursed her son, and how she spat on them and sent them away. I told you how Albina walked home through that day and night, right after giving birth to her baby, Shida, and I told you how Albina gave up her medicine pouch.

"Well, what I didn't tell you is what a terrible mistake all of that was. That old woman was wrong, Shida. Albina hadn't cursed her husband. She shouldn't have blamed herself for failing to heal Milembe. She was giving birth to their baby when he died. People die, Shida. It doesn't matter what kind of fancy pills or herbs or medicine men you have. Sometimes people die, and we can't help that.

"You know, after Albina gave away her medicine pouch, she slowly realized that she couldn't be blamed for Milembe's death. But what about all those villagers who had come to her, asking to be healed, after her return to Litongo? She turned them away, Shida. And after that, people didn't even bother asking her for help. They knew she wouldn't give it."

Shida looked up at Mama. Mama's face looked clear, clear of the veil of sadness that had been draped over it for years now. Her eyes were sharp and pleading — they almost seemed to reach out to her, begging Shida not to drown in the despair that she knew all too well.

"Because of one death, Shida . . ." Mama pulled her daughter into her lap. "Because of one death, Albina failed to heal others and that, that was Albina's only curse. Furaha's death might rip you apart, but you have to tie on that pouch and stand up and force yourself to keep healing until the day when you can finally forgive yourself and realize that you didn't kill Furaha. Nobody did, Shida."

Shida stared up at Mama. She couldn't remember when Mama had last held her like this.

"You heard me, Shida. Go and pick up that pouch. Don't waste any time. You've got Babu and Grace and many other people who need to be healed waiting for you."

Shida leaned over to push herself up, but her foot caught on the edge of her skirt. She stumbled. Four hands reached out and caught her.

"Shida, remember," the nurse said, "my pills aren't magic. Sometimes they work and sometimes they don't. For all we know, your *mamihigo* treatment is more effective than my quinine, and God knows you have a special touch. Say the words, Shida. Tell us out loud that you are a healer."

"I . . ." Shida's voice was a raspy mess of tears and mucus.

Mama's warm hands grasped Shida's shoulders, and then her face — clear and strong — appeared in front of Shida once more. "You are a healer, Shida. Say it."

"I . . . I am a healer." Shida croaked.

"Again."

"I am a healer."

"Good," Mama said. "Now go get your medicine pouch."

Shida's feet shuffled forward.

Chapter 18

Do not step on the dog's tail, and he will not bite you.
— *Cameroonian proverb*

"The witch must be responsible for this!" one man yelled over the crowd. "She didn't even come to the funeral. Sukuma people don't miss funerals, unless they're the ones who cursed the dead."

Men and women swarmed around Babu outside Mama Grace's hut. Shida had just come back from the fields with Mama and the nurse. She sidled up next to Grace in the yard.

"Mama Malongo?" Shida asked quietly.

Grace nodded.

"We can't know for sure." Babu was hunched over, and when he lifted his head, Shida could see circles under his eyes. "The young medicine man assures me the curse came from my ancestors. They were angry at me for moving the village here and leaving our old homes."

The gathering rumbled and then one woman spoke up. It was Mama Nganza. "Please don't think I'm being disrespectful, Grandfather. But the young medicine man hasn't gained the wisdom of age. Just because he suggests the poor child was cursed by something else, we can't be sure about the witch. If the old *mganga* who stayed behind in Litongo said the curse was something else, then I'd believe him. But at the moment, we can't be sure."

Voices hummed in agreement.

"I have one question for all of you." A woman at the opposite side of the crowd spoke up. "How can you say for sure that Mama Malongo is a witch?"

Shida's eyes widened. The woman stood tall and spoke confidently, but she was unmistakably Mama.

"How dare she say the witch's name so soon after the child's death?" one man said.

"Who is she to question us? She, herself — "

Babu cleared his voice. "My friends, it seems we have come to a dire time. We have lost dear Furaha, and we are feeling unsure of our place in this new home. I hate to do this, but I think it's time we call the old *mganga*. I will send two boys with my bicycle to Litongo. I know he didn't want to make the move to this new village. But the boys can push him here and back on my bicycle. The old man will understand — this is an emergency. In the meantime, no one should approach Mama Malongo or her compound. Can we agree to that?"

Whispers filled the compound.

"We can agree to that," one man said.

Other voices joined him. "We can agree."

As the crowd dispersed, Shida and Grace ducked into Mama Grace's hut. Someone had removed Furaha's bed and two new cowhide mats were laid out on the floor. Grace lay down on the side of one and then she patted the other side.

"You want me to sleep here?" Shida said.

Grace nodded. She still wasn't speaking.

Shida felt the familiar shame flood over her again — maybe Grace blamed Shida. Maybe that's why she wasn't speaking. Grace hadn't heard what the nurse said about her pills sometimes not working. But then Shida remembered Mama's face looking at her, pleading with her, telling her that she couldn't give up. Grace wouldn't ask Shida to sleep by her if she thought Shida had killed Furaha. Shida steeled herself and swallowed the lump in her throat. "Let me go tell Mama then."

Shida ran outside and looked around the yard, but Mama's familiar faded red *kitenge* was not in the dwindling crowd. Shida's eyes scanned up the road and then stopped. There was Mama, holding Babu's arm, leading him as he hobbled home.

Shida hurried up behind them.

Mama was talking. "You can't blame yourself, Father. Sometimes bad things happen that we can't explain." She looked up to the hills toward Litongo. The sun was setting and the sky was awash with streaks of pink and orange. "Look, Father. The sun knows you've brought us to the right home. The ancestors may not know this is home yet, but the sun knows."

Shida stopped in her tracks. Her body flooded with a warmth that came not from the fading sunlight, but from Mama's words. Shida closed her eyes and allowed herself to bask in the feeling for a moment. So Mama was home. Mama was home, at last, in more ways than one.

✕✕✕✕✕✕✕✕✕✕✕✕✕✕✕

At the first sign of light the next morning, Shida stole out of Grace's hut. She'd been awake a good portion of the night, thinking about Furaha and worrying about Grace's silence and the old *mganga*'s visit.

Shida had no place to go. It was a Saturday and there was no school. But she could go out to Mama's plot and check on their cassava.

Shida crossed a corner of Babu's maize field. The plants waved a quiet hello. She jogged between two fields of bobbing sweet potatoes. When she finally neared Mama's plot, Shida spotted a woman hunching over it.

191

The woman turned around. "I see you're still running around."

It was Mama Malongo. She held her back with one hand and a cup in the other. "Come over here," she said. "I won't hurt you. You should know that with a mama like yours. I hear they've called the *mganga* from Litongo to accuse me of killing the little girl child."

Shida's bare feet stuck to the sandy earth.

"I was sorry to hear about the little girl. I watched her pass by on the road and she always seemed like a good child. A couple of weeks ago, she wandered into my yard to play. I don't think she knew who I was. Children are afraid of my name, but most don't know what I look like. The first day little Furaha wandered onto my compound, she gathered sticks and bark from the woods and made little toy houses around the yard. After she was finished, she danced around the houses and made up a song about a village. I told her she could come back, and she did. A few times."

"Furaha?" Shida stammered. "You mean Furaha built those little spirit houses in your yard?"

Mama Malongo huffed out a short laugh. "Spirit houses? Those were just a little girl's play houses, not spirit houses." She squinted at Shida. "You didn't really think I was a witch, did you?"

"I, uh . . ." Shida pulled at the edge of her blouse. "No, I don't think you're a witch."

"But you used to think it." The old woman turned and dipped her cup into a bucket. She poured one cupful of water after another along several delicate rows of seedlings.

Shida watched. No one else bothered to carry water out this far to water crops.

"Your mother just planted seeds for her herbs this morning," said Mama Malongo. "When your grandfather called the two of us together and asked us to plant herbs as good medicine to help his family, she refused, but it seems the little girl's death has made her reconsider."

"Mama — planting herbs?" Shida said. But there, past Mama Malongo's small, dry plot, and past the ridges of dirt where Shida and Mama had planted cassava tubers, were three newly hoed and watered rows. "I didn't know you were a . . ." Shida stared at Mama Malongo.

"A healer? Yes." Mama Malongo smiled. "You, young healer, should know there were other female healers before you in Litongo, and not just your mama. For many years, I was respected as a healer of pregnant women and small babies. Your mother worked with me when she was your age. But then bad things befell both of us. We each lost a husband and, in my case, a child. People stopped calling me to their homes after that. Except, of course, your Babu. He's asked me to help with small projects every now and then, like these." Mama Malongo pointed to her seedlings.

The old woman turned back to watering her herbs. She

was careful not to drown the plants, and after every cupful of water, she stopped to pull small weeds and to create little rings around her seedlings to hold the water.

"What will you do when the old *mganga* comes?"

Mama Malongo grabbed a cloth bundle from the corner of her plot and placed it in her bucket. She picked up the bucket, bracing her back, and turned to Shida. "I'm headed into the hills for a couple of days. I'll return after people have calmed down. This isn't the first time I've been blamed for something that wasn't my fault. My husband's relatives were certain I'd killed him, but after some time, they forgot."

"But what will you eat?" Shida said.

"I have a bundle of sweet potatoes in my bucket here." Mama Malongo swung her head back toward her heavy load with the slowness of someone whose body had taught her to do nothing too sudden. "Your Babu gave me these." The old woman hobbled along the side of Mama and Shida's plot, out toward the hills.

Shida leaned toward Mama Malongo. "Go — " Shida's voice cracked. "Go peacefully, Mama Malongo."

Mama Malongo turned and smiled. "Stay peacefully, young healer."

Chapter 19

There is no medicine to cure hatred.
— *Ghanaian proverb*

The old *mganga* came rolling in on Babu's bicycle early that evening. The two boys who had been sent to collect him pulled the bike to a stop outside of Mama Grace's hut. Three men lifted the old man off.

"You've traveled far to visit us," Babu said. "We're honored to have you and thank you for coming, my friend."

The *mganga* hobbled toward Babu and took his hand. Their watery eyes met.

"I'm very sorry, very sorry for the loss of your girl."

Babu nodded. "We're also sorry. She wasn't ready." He clenched his lips together, and for a moment they quivered, but then Babu straightened his face and looked up. "Tell me, what is the news of Litongo? What's the news of your sons and the other families who remain there?"

The old men continued to greet one another, asking about the news of the other's farming and homes. They were being polite. The real news would come once they went inside Mama Grace's hut and had some time to eat and talk.

For the next two hours, Uncle Bujiko's wives shuttled food in and out of the little hut while villagers congregated in the yard. Shida joined Grace where she sat outside, still silent.

When Babu finally emerged from the hut, the crowd grew quiet.

"My children," Babu said. "We're very honored to have the respected *mganga* here with us today. He served us well in Litongo and he's been very generous to join us in this time of need."

The faces staring back at Babu looked stern.

"Unfortunately, the last few months have been very hard on the *mganga*. He's aged significantly and I believe he made a good decision to stay in Litongo. It's his time now to rest."

People's heads turned. There were a few whispers.

"Is the old man still with us?" one man said.

"Oh, yes," Babu said. "He's resting inside Mama Grace's hut right now — but his thoughts are slowing down. His mind is tired."

"You have to tell us what you mean, Babu."

"I mean to say . . ." Babu shifted his walking stick from one hand to the other. "I'm afraid the questions we're asking are too much for the old *mganga*. He's saying something about buried clothes. He's a very good man, but I don't think we're concerned about any clothes."

Uncle Magema lifted his head from the crowd. "Father, please know that I respect your opinion, but the *mganga* has come all this way and he's helped us greatly in the past. Shouldn't we just give him a chance to make sense of the situation, even if nothing comes of it?"

Other voices hummed in agreement.

Babu moved his cane to his other hand and leaned forward on it so far Shida was afraid he might fall. "I understand what you're saying. I'll call him out, but we must keep in mind that he may be too tired to help us."

Babu brought out the *mganga*. Two villagers hurried to the old man and offered their arms for support. The *mganga* strained to tilt his head up, looking toward the edge of Uncle Bujiko's compound near the candelabra tree. "Take me there." His voice was a hoarse whisper, but the whole crowd shuffled forward with him. When he stopped, two boys ran over with chairs and the old men settled into them.

The *mganga* looked at Kulwa, Uncle Bujiko's son.

Shida could see the old man's tongue move and his vocal cords strain in his neck as if he were trying to force words to escape his chest. "Bring me a hoe, my son."

Several hands pushed the little boy toward his mother's hut.

"Bring the *mganga* a good hoe, boy."

"Go quickly."

The crowd's eyes followed Kulwa across the compound and back again. The young boy leaned the handle of a large *jembe* hoe against the *mganga*'s legs.

"All of the young ones of my friend here, those who come from the wombs of his daughters or the wives of his sons . . ." The *mganga* strained to look up, but his bent neck refused to straighten, so he placed his palm on Babu's leg. "All of my friend's young ones who go to school, line up in front of me."

People whispered and looked away.

"All of my grandchildren who go to the school, line up in front of us," Babu said.

There was a rustling in the crowd, but soon all of Babu's school-age grandchildren stood in front of the two elders. Shida and Grace positioned themselves at one end of the line. The adults in the crowd and the unrelated children moved back into the road.

The *mganga* lifted his shaking head and grunted. "Boys, step back," he said.

The boys stepped back.

The old man nodded. "Each of you girls come up to the hoe and spit on the blade."

No one moved. Shida shifted her weight between her feet. What was the *mganga* up to? She looked at Babu.

He nodded.

She walked up to the hoe and spat. The white, foamy liquid ran down the dull metal. As Shida walked back to her place in line, Grace passed her, and soon all of their female cousins were huddled around the two older girls, having spat on the blade.

"Now," the old man said. "Have one of your sons, my friend" — he brushed Babu's leg — "have one of them dig in front of that cactus over there with this hoe." Babu studied the old man, but then turned and waved at his youngest son, Uncle Magema.

The thin young man strode up to the hoe and began digging in front of the cactus.

Dirt piled up.

People began to whisper.

"The old *mganga's* tired."

"How will this help us stop the witch?"

But as Uncle Magema raised the hoe to swing it back down into the earth, he stopped. "There's something here."

A group of men knelt around the hole. "It's cloth," one said. The crowd leaned in as the men scraped dirt away with their fingers.

One of the men stood up with something in his hands. He walked over to Babu and handed it to him. Babu stared at the bundle of cloth in his lap and then he flinched. "Shida." His hands were shaking. "Shida!"

"Yes, Babu." Shida crouched in front of him.

"It's your yellow dress, Shida. It's here."

Shida picked up the ball and turned it in the air in front of her. There was the sleeve of her yellow dress.

"That's my daughter's shirt!" one of Shida's aunts shouted.

"And that's my girl's skirt!" another said.

Shida's hands began to shake, but another pair of hands met hers on the cloth ball.

It was Grace. Grace took the wad of clothes and began to unravel it. First came Shida's yellow dress, and then Furaha's pink blouse, and then Grace's purple dress, and another little cousin's blue dress, until there was a long chain of clothes.

Grace handed the chain to the *mganga*.

The old man ran his fingers over each piece of clothing and then nodded his head. "You see. Someone has put a curse on your family for educating these girls." He lifted up Furaha's pink blouse. It was riddled with holes. "This one, this is the shirt of the little one who's gone. It was eaten by insects, which completed the curse."

The crowd gasped. Shida wrapped her arms around Grace, but Grace stood stone still.

"With time, the others' clothes would have been eaten," the *mganga* said. "Then the curse would have been complete for them as well."

"But who cursed these children?" Uncle Magema said. His daughter was gripping his leg.

A sea of faces turned to the old *mganga*, but he was swinging his head back and forth, as if he were swaying to some deep, slow rhythm. "All I can say is that whoever buried these clothes caused little Furaha's death."

"Please, old man," someone in the crowd said. "You must help us. We've had many problems since we moved here and we must learn who has cursed us."

The gathering hummed.

The old man gripped the arms of his chair, as if he were going to push himself up, but then he slumped back. He rested his hands in his lap. "I'll tell you, but wait until to-morrow. First, I must rest."

"How could you?" A voice boomed from the back of the gathering.

The crowd parted and Uncle Bujiko appeared. He was flailing his arms and clawing toward the *mganga*. "How could you?"

A group of men circled him. They grabbed him around the middle and pulled down his arms. "Be calm," they said.

"He'll tell us tomorrow."

"We know you're grieving for the little one. We know you're ready to go find the witch, but we must give the old man time."

Uncle Bujiko struggled in their arms, but he was overpowered and began to moan. "How could you? How could you?"

"Poor man," a woman next to Shida said. "He's lost his daughter and now he must wait to hear who has cursed her. Who can blame him for being angry at the witch?"

But Shida was watching Uncle Bujiko. He wasn't looking around wildly. He wasn't hunting the crowd for Mama Malongo or scanning the sky for her owl. His eyes were directed straight at the *mganga,* and he looked angrier than she had ever seen him before.

Chapter 20

When spider webs unite, they can tie up a lion.
— *Ethiopian proverb*

Someone grabbed her shoulders and Shida felt herself being yanked up before she was completely awake. The midnight air was balmy, but the mud floor beneath her feet felt cool. Shida shivered and looked around.

Mama Grace and Uncle Bujiko's youngest wife were asleep on the floor of Grace's hut, but Grace was standing in front of Shida with the door ajar.

"What's going on?" Shida said.

Grace pulled Shida outside and pointed to a light on the other side of Uncle Bujiko's cattle corral. It was streaming from under the metal door of Mama Kulwa's house.

"Is your father alright?" Shida said.

Grace nodded as she led Shida up to the house.

"Mama Kulwa?"

But Grace bypassed the front door and walked around the side of the house.

A dry leaf crackled under Shida's foot and Grace turned back and scowled. At the back of the house, she pointed up to a small window.

"How could you let this happen?" Uncle Bujiko said from inside.

"I told you there would be risks." Shida could just make out the hoarse voice of an old man. "There are always risks."

Shida grabbed Grace's arm. The *mganga* was supposed to be sleeping in Uncle Bujiko's youngest wife's hut. That's why the young woman was sleeping at Mama Grace's tonight.

"What!" Uncle Bujiko boomed. "Risks? Nothing like this!"

"But you agreed to do whatever it would take," the *mganga* said. "Remember how badly you wanted them to return to Litongo. I'm very sorry about the girl, but I warned you magic is never clean."

"Magic! MAGIC! Are you saying you made *me* do magic?"

"Wait, my son. Tell me. Did you take the necessary steps?"

"Yes, of course, I let the cows out, but — "

"And did you put the amulet of the eldest girl's dead father on the foreigner's door?"

"Yes, I put it on the teacher's compound, but no one noticed, so I shifted it to the witch's."

"And what about the poison dust? You were only supposed to put the dust on the crops, not on any food."

"You idiot. The dust is fertilizer. It's for food. The government gave it to us to help grow crops. Too much can kill the crops, not people."

"Be calm, my son. I don't know about this fertilizer. And you buried the clothes?"

"Old man, don't make me angry. You saw the buried clothes. I've done everything, but you lied to me. None of this was supposed to be magic. I don't know magic. I just wanted to scare them back to Litongo."

"You came to a medicine man, my son. Of course you expected magic. I told you before we started, magic is never clean. I said there might be risks for you, or the village, or your family. But you were certain they had to return to Litongo. You were worried about the cattle you left behind in Litongo to graze, and you said your daughters would become big-headed in this school — you said they'd all end up like your sister. You wanted to save them. You wanted to save all of Litongo. You said you'd do *anything*."

"What?" Uncle Bujiko screamed. "I can't believe you!

I never meant to hurt any of them. I . . . I never agreed to kill Furaha." Choked sobbing drifted out the window, along with the thumps of pacing feet. "I've had it with this place. We really must be cursed. I'm going to finish this off myself." The metal door slammed at the front of the house.

A pool of light swung along the path leading to Uncle Bujiko's fields. In the middle of the light, Uncle Bujiko clutched a lantern in one hand and a cloth bag in the other.

"He's going to go poison his crops with fertilizer," Shida said.

But Grace was already running, tearing across the dark yard. For a second, all Shida could do was watch. Grace's pale palms flicked back behind her as she ran. And then Shida was sprinting after her.

Shida grabbed Grace's shoulders at the edge of the compound, but Grace jerked herself free. Shida dove for her cousin's waist and tackled her to the ground. Grace lunged and leapt, pawing at the earth, until Shida overwhelmed her and Grace finally grew limp.

The night was dark again, and quiet, except for the girls' heavy breathing.

"I'm sorry, Grace," Shida said, "but you can't follow him right now. He might hurt you." Shida lifted herself up onto her hands and knees, still straddling her cousin.

Grace turned over in the dirt. She took a deep breath and then something erupted inside of her. She began sobbing, but not silently this time. Her moans seemed to fill the compound.

"Grace, even if we catch him killing his plants with fertilizer, we're just two young girls. No one will believe us."

"Then what can we do, Shida?" Grace pushed herself up, forcing Shida back on her knees. "He killed her, Shida. He killed Furaha."

"Oh, Grace. I'm so sorry." Shida wrapped her arms around her cousin. "I'm so sorry Furaha's gone and I'm so sorry about your father. It sounds like he let out the cows and did all these other things to scare us, but I don't think he killed Furaha."

Grace sniffled loudly. "How can you say that, Shida?"

"The nurse said she had a bad case of malaria, Grace. Furaha said her arms and legs were aching. Maybe your father thinks he killed Furaha. Maybe he thinks the medicine man did it, but I'm pretty sure Furaha died of malaria."

Shida leaned back on her knees to look at Grace. Grace shuddered, but the tears were no longer running down her face. "We've got to catch him, Shida."

A few minutes later, Shida was leaning over her grandfather's cowhide bed and shaking his shoulder. "Babu . . . Babu."

The old man opened his eyes slowly and stared up at Shida.

"Babu, it's Uncle Bujiko." Shida gasped for air. "He was talking to the *mganga* . . . Uncle Bujiko put father's amulets on Mama Malongo and the teacher's compounds . . . Uncle Bujiko buried the clothes . . . I don't think he killed Furaha, but he wanted to scare us . . . He's going to poison the food crops now . . . We have to catch him!"

Babu was still lying on the floor, but Shida could see his eyes take in everything. "I understand what you're saying, daughter. I'll start walking toward Bujiko's fields as fast as I can, but you must wake up your mother and have her come with you on my bicycle. I'm too old to ride it now and your mother's eyes will serve as mine."

"Mama?" Shida said. "But no one will believe Mama."

"Your mother needs this, Shida," Babu said. "She can speak for me, and people will believe me. Go and take my bicycle to your mother."

Mama jumped on the bicycle and struggled to pedal through the deep sand, but once she made her way to the middle of the road, the girls had to lengthen their strides to keep up. Just before the water pump, they passed Babu. He was hobbling down the road, gripping his walking stick. "Go quickly, my daughters! You're helping our village. You're helping all of Tanzania."

They ran right through Uncle Bujiko's compound. When they reached the low wall of Uncle Bujiko's maize plants, Mama dropped the bike. "Which way?" She turned to the two girls.

Way off in the distance, Shida spotted a light. She raced toward it, zigzagging and jumping over lines of maize plants, until she was standing in a plot of spinach. Just beyond was Uncle Bujiko. His broad shoulders jerked as he flung handfuls of fertilizer out over a patch of tomatoes.

"Uncle Bujiko, we know what you're doing!" Shida yelled. "We know you're poisoning these tomatoes, just like you've been poisoning Babu's maize, and the village's cotton."

The huge man swung around and jerked his head, trying to pinpoint the source of the voice, but he was blinded by his bright lantern.

"Who are you? Where are you?"

A pair of hands gripped Shida's shoulders and then slid off. Mama stepped into the light.

Uncle Bujiko's jaw clenched.

"Stop, Bujiko," Mama said. "How is it worth doing any of this, just to go back to all of your cattle and your large farm in Litongo? So what if the girls are in school? Perhaps they'll have more of a chance than your poor sister did."

"My poor sister — " Uncle Bujiko lunged at Mama, hurling a handful of fertilizer.

"Cover your eyes, Mama!" Shida squeezed her own eyes shut, and jumped toward her mother.

"You were never my poor sister," Uncle Bujiko said.

"You were always out running around with that silly medicine pouch of yours while I was left to stay with the old ladies at home."

"Stop!" A woman's voice cut through the night like a machete.

Uncle Bujiko froze and Mama and Shida swung around.

"How could you do this? How could you kill her?" Grace stepped into the light.

Uncle Bujiko stumbled backwards.

"How could you kill your own daughter just to get your old fields and grazing land back? How can you call yourself a father?"

Uncle Bujiko's face softened. "I didn't do it, Grace. The old man never said we were doing magic. Someone must have cursed her. Someone . . ." Bujiko's eyes locked on Shida. "What about her? What about Shida? People said she was healing Furaha, but when she left that night, Furaha got worse. Maybe she's the one. Maybe she cursed Furaha."

Grace shook her hands at her father. "How dare you accuse Shida? Why do people like you always have to get others in trouble by talking about curses?" Grace fell to her knees, sobbing.

Uncle Bujiko kneeled down in front of Grace. "Grace, I didn't kill her. Please believe me."

Grace trembled. "It doesn't matter if I believe you. If Furaha had lived, you wouldn't have wanted her to go to school. You would have wanted her to work in your fields and then get married to a man no better than you. You wouldn't have given her a good life anyway."

"Oh Grace, can't you see I was trying to bring us back to our good lives in Litongo?" Uncle Bujiko reached out to grip Grace's arm, trying to make eye contact with her.

But Grace only turned away.

"Grace, we couldn't have survived here," Uncle Bujiko pleaded. "This collective farming is nonsense. We wouldn't have had enough food to eat. In Litongo I worked hard to be a respected man. I had pasture to keep enough cows to give you and your mother milk every day. In Litongo, you weren't confused with this school nonsense. How could we find you a husband with you going to school? A good man expects his wife to — "

The sound of metal rattling behind them caused everyone to turn.

Heavy breathing, mixed with the creak of an unoiled bicycle. Uncle Magema, Babu's youngest son, pedaled into the light with Babu balanced on the back of his bike. Shida, Grace, and Mama ran toward the bicycle to steady Babu. Grace lifted his leg up over the frame while Mama and Shida braced his body and gently lowered him to the ground.

"We caught him throwing fertilizer, Babu." Shida turned to point to her uncle, but nothing but bright light glared back at her.

Grace stumbled into the light, trampling plants. "Babu . . . Babu, he was just here." She turned around, panic flashing across her face. "Babu, I promise. I can run after him."

Babu hobbled over to her. "I believe you, Grace. I've always believed you, and your cousin Shida." Babu shook his head, looking down at a pile of fertilizer at his feet. "Your father has been hurting since he was a young child, Grace. He was sickly and jealous, and though his body recovered with age, the jealousy never disappeared. He's continued to feel like a weak little boy who needs to prove himself, even if that means hurting others. That's not what we need here in this village. We need to let him go, Grace. "

Grace pounded her fists down against a tomato plant. "I hate him, Babu. I hate him so much."

Babu placed his hands on Grace's closely-cropped hair, pouring the last of his energy into his granddaughter. Mama and Shida clutched each of Grace's shaking shoulders.

"Let him go, child," Babu said. "Let him go."

Chapter 21

If you educate a woman, you educate a nation.
— *Liberian proverb*

An hour after sunrise, a crowd had gathered on Uncle Bujiko's compound. Shida stood with Grace behind Babu's chair, waiting for the crowd to quiet down. Her eyes felt heavy. They had had a long night. Grace had recounted everything they had heard between Uncle Bujiko and the *mganga*, and once Babu knew the full story, he had insisted that Uncle Magema get the *mganga* out of town before daylight. Babu was afraid the villagers would be upset with the old man if they learned of his role in advising Uncle Bujiko.

Shida scanned the sun-drenched hillside behind the whispering crowd. Just below the top of the hill, she thought she saw a moving speck. Shida smiled. Uncle Magema had moved quickly, pushing the old man over the hills on his bicycle. The speck disappeared over the peak, and Babu cleared his voice.

"My friends, today I have some answers for you. In fact, I believe I've been given all of the answers we need to understand our position in this new village of ours. Much has happened this night. I've learned who released our cattle, who poisoned our crops, and how my granddaughters' clothes were buried."

Whispers ran through the crowd.

"We all feel deep sadness to have lost our little Furaha. She was a joyful little girl, but I now believe she died naturally."

The faces in front of Shida frowned in disbelief.

"We all know people who have been cursed by bad medicine or by ancestors who weren't happy with them. At first, when I believed our village had suffered from a string of curses, I was convinced that little Furaha was just one more victim in a series of bad medicine. But now I'm relieved to know that Furaha wasn't cursed. Our nurse here in Njia Panda says she knows of the disease that killed Furaha, and I believe she's right."

A man in the front of the crowd opened his mouth. Shida gripped Grace's hand. But for the first time in Shida's life, Babu just kept talking.

"Last night, my son Magema, my daughter Albina, these two young ladies" — Babu pointed behind himself — "and I found the person who has been causing us all of our problems. A few of us overheard this person talking with the old *mganga*. This person admitted to letting out our cows soon after we had all arrived and this person also talked about poisoning our cotton fields. Later, we found this same person in his own fields, poisoning his tomato plants. He was, in short, trying to make us all believe that we were cursed and needed to leave Njia Panda."

Faces in the crowd started to turn. "Who is this, Babu?"

"The person, I am sad to say, is my own son . . . Bujiko."

Jaws dropped.

"Why would Bujiko kill the cotton he'd worked so hard on?" one man said.

"How did he kill the plants?"

"What about the witch?"

Babu tried to answer each question carefully, but eventually he stopped. "Let me start at the beginning," he said. And he did. He reminded people of the sickly little boy Bujiko had been. He described how he had watched Bujiko's body grow strong, but his ambition remain tainted with jealousy. Bujiko always had a need to prove that he was better and stronger than everyone else, and the spirit of Njia Panda — of taking care of each other — made it hard for him to stand out. So Bujiko released all of New Njia Panda's cattle one night and placed Shida's father's amulet first on the property of the teacher and then of Mama Malongo, in order to lead the new villagers to believe they were cursed. He over-applied fertilizer from the community shed to burn the village's cotton. "Finally," Babu said, "Bujiko stole my granddaughters' clothes to make it seem that someone had cursed them for attending school."

"So where is Bujiko now?" a man said from the back of the crowd. "What does he have to say for himself? He's caused us a lot of grief."

"He's gone." Babu sighed. "He ran away last night when we caught him poisoning his own tomatoes."

The crowd rumbled.

Babu rested his forehead on the end of his walking stick. "I imagine this doesn't change what I know you've all been thinking — that we should return to Litongo."

The crowd grew silent.

"Return to Litongo, Babu?" Mama Lewanga stepped forward. "I'd rather stay here. The nurse has given my boy a mosquito net to sleep under and he hasn't been sick since. With her care and Shida's, I can imagine my boy growing into a man here."

"Yes, Babu." A man Shida recognized as an important farmer and trader from Litongo spoke up. "Now that we know no one has been cursing us, we have to give Njia

Panda a second chance. Sure, living here is an adjustment — our houses are all crammed together in the village, and some of us have to walk great distances to farm, but this experience has taught us that we must think beyond just ourselves. All of Tanzania and Africa are watching us from afar. The *wazungu* no longer rule over us. Nyerere is our president. He is asking us to come together and to work as an extended family, just as our ancestors once did. Even when we lost poor Furaha, I doubted the ancestors were against our moving — more likely they are looking upon us and smiling. If we can make this village work, if we can truly live like brothers and sisters, then we can proudly call ourselves Sukuma."

Voices murmured in agreement.

"What you say is true, my friend," Babu said. "And I have learned something else from this experience: the value of educating our girls. It was because of my granddaughter Shida's connections to the nurse that we learned what caused little Furaha's death, and it was two of our school-educated girls, Grace and Shida, who understood that putting too much fertilizer on a plant could kill it. Many sadnesses have befallen us since this move, but already I can see one benefit — our children are learning good things in this school."

Shida waited for voices to rise in the crowd, but instead, she watched eyebrows rise, one after another, in simple, silent agreement. The sun peeked up over a tree and flooded the compound in light.

"We're sorry to see that you've lost a grandchild and a son in just a few days, Babu," Mama Nganza said.

Baby Lewanga's father walked up to Babu and took his hand. "We're sorry, Grandfather, very sorry." Soon a line of villagers lead up to Babu to give him their condolences, just as they had a few days ago to Mama Grace. Shida felt a lump rise in her throat. Her eyes welled up with tears — of course the villagers were offering Babu their condolences, but they were also telling him that they still trusted him, that they did not blame him for his son's injustices, that his dream was now, perhaps more than ever, theirs.

Someone nudged Shida's arm. "You young women did good work." It was Baby Lewanga's father. The line of villagers was following him from Babu to Grace and Shida.

"Your education at the school has been good for all of us," Mama Lewanga said.

"You girls did well," Mama Nganza said. "You're lucky to have this school. The ancestors have been good to me. I have a nice husband and enough food, but I've never learned to read or write. It's good you're learning."

"Thank you," Shida said.

And then Mama Nganza looked behind Shida. "You've raised a good daughter, Mama Shida. You should be proud."

After all of New Njia Panda had congratulated Shida and Grace, and after Babu had taken a nap in Mama Grace's hut, Shida led her aunt and cousin and grandfather back to Babu's compound, where Mama had promised them she would have lunch ready. But when they reached the compound, the yard was silent.

Shida peeked into Mama's hut. It was empty. She looked into the cooking hut. There was no one there. An old, familiar disappointment rose in Shida as she turned to apologize to her guests, but then she heard something. Voices were coming from the sky. Shida looked up. Bright blue shone down, but also voices.

They came from the top of her kopje.

Shida ran toward the big granite rock, still looking up. The voices got clearer.

"Oh, yes. We have some very famous Sukuma stories. The most famous is the story of Masala Kulangwa. People say he was a young boy, but I believe that Masala Kulangwa was a girl. She saved her village, just like Shida and Grace did for us today."

"Mama?" Shida said. She turned to Babu.

The old man's back was hunched more than usual, but his mouth was stretched wide with an enormous grin.

The name Masala Kulangwa seemed to dance through the air, bringing the yard alive. The colors of the mango tree and laundry hanging on the cattle corral glowed; the walls of their mud huts softened, as if with age; and Shida was flooded with a sense of home.

"You're here!" Mama stood at the edge of the giant kopje, just behind the tiny spirit house. She looked taller, and her hair was neatly tucked into her headscarf.

"Come over here to the kopje. Nurse Goldfilda and I brought lunch up. Everything's ready. I want you to come, too, Father. I've borrowed one of Bujiko's ladders for you to climb up."

Shida hiccupped.

"Come on, Shida!" Mama said. "You'll need some food in your belly to stop those hiccups."

Shida took one of Babu's hands and led him over to the base of her kopje. She stepped up a few ladder rungs and reached down to him. Mama Grace and Grace braced him from behind.

But Babu's back straightened out and his limbs loosened. He hopped up the two rungs to Shida, and before she knew it, Shida had jumped up the remaining rungs to be out of his way.

When they all reached the top, Shida turned to look at her mother. At her feet was the spirit house, and next to that, a spread of food — rice, chicken, spinach, and tomato sauce. Next to her was the nurse with her hands on her hips, just like Mama. And behind Mama, the village of Njia Panda stretched out with the school and clinic looming large in the middle, surrounded by lines of huts, and rings of fields.

"What a feast you've made for us!" Grace said.

"Amazing!" Mama Grace said.

Mama's beautiful white teeth shone back at them through a grin.

"What a home!" Babu said. He was standing up straight, surveying the view.

Shida bit her lower lip, trying to hold back the tears she felt brimming in her eyes. Babu was right — this was their home. They had finally arrived. Here Shida was on her very own Sukuma pyramid. A few things were different from her dream. Shida stood at the top now. Instead of water, beautiful huts and papaya, mango, and flamboyant trees surrounded her. Shida didn't have to save any children up above — Furaha was beyond saving — but perhaps she and Grace had saved Mama. And, in a way, Mama had helped to save them.

Shida walked over to Mama and wrapped her arms around her mother's waist. "We're home, Mama. We've finally found ourselves a home."

Mama's arms squeezed Shida back.

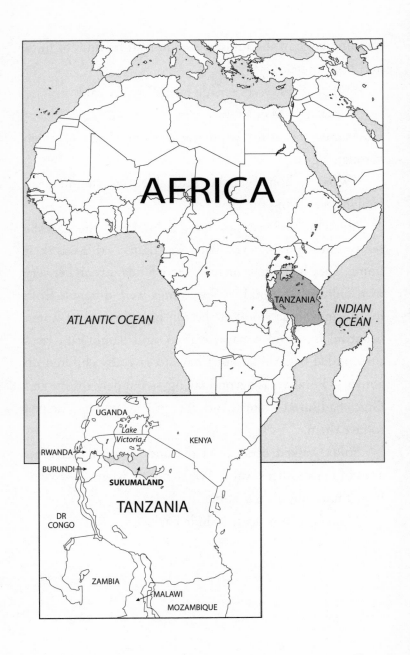

Glossary

Babu — grandfather (Swahili)

> *Babu* is also a term of respect. In Tanzania, if you don't know an older man's name, it's acceptable to call him *Babu*.

Baraka — blessing (Swahili)

> This is a common name for boys. President Obama's first name is derived from this word.

Candelabra tree — a succulent plant (English)

> This tree looks like a cactus with long branches arching up like a candle holder, or candelabra. The sap is toxic and can cause burns or even blindness.

Ehh — yes (Sukuma/Swahili)

> This is a sound that Swahili and Sukuma speakers use often to mean "yes," much the way an English speaker might say "uh-huh."

Flamboyant tree — a tropical tree with distinctive red flowers (English)

Flamboyant trees have fern-like leaves and showy red flowers. There is a flamboyant tree behind Shida on the cover of this book, and two other flamboyant trees feature prominently in the story.

Furaha — happiness (Swahili)

Furaha is sometimes used as a girl's name in Tanzania.

Jembe — a large hoe used as a shovel (Swahili)

In Tanzania, people do most of their digging with *jembes*. About 85% of Tanzanians are involved in farming; most Tanzanians spend part of each day at their family's farm. Below is a young woman using a *jembe*.

Kitenge — traditional clothing worn by Tanzanian women (Swahili)

Kitenge come in sets of two identical rectangles, usually printed in bright colors. They can be wrapped around the waist as skirts, or tied on as shirts, headscarves, or even baby carriers, as the woman below has done.

Kopje — granite outcroppings, particularly those found in Africa (English, derived from Afrikaans)

The kopjes in Sukumaland are particularly impressive — they sometimes look like enormous boulders balanced one on top of the other in what appear to be totally precarious formations, or like rock walls jutting out of the earth, as in the picture below.

Kwa heri — good-bye (Swahili)

Kwa means "with" and *heri* means "blessing" or "luck," so when Swahili speakers say good-bye, they are wishing each other good fortune.

Maasai — an East African tribe

The Maasai people are well known for living around Tanzania's famous parks, like the Serengeti, and for their beautiful dress, including intricate bead work and bright red wrap clothes. Their lives center on cattle, which is why Shida mentions them when her village's cattle are let loose.

Mama — mother (Swahili)

Mama is the prefix for a woman's name in Tanzania, much like Ms. or Mrs. in English. When a woman has her first child, her name becomes *Mama* + her baby's name. So when Shida was born not only was she given an unfortunate name — so was her mother.

Mamihigo — tree used for treating malaria (Sukuma)

The Sukuma boil the bark of the *mamihigo* tree in water and then either shower with it, inhale the steam, or drink it. Tanzanians continue to use traditional medicines like *mamihigo* as well as pills they can buy at the pharmacy, but for many people the pharmaceutical pills are too expensive.

Mayu — mother (Sukuma)

Shida calls Mama Lewanga *Mayu* when she is trying to comfort her at the nurse's clinic. Her choice to use Sukuma, rather than Swahili, might have helped Mama Lewanga feel more comfortable.

Mganga — medicine man (Swahili)

In traditional Sukuma culture, medicine men and women were the doctors. They used herbs, amulets (like Milembe's bell necklace), and special connections with ancestors to heal people.

Mrefu — tall (Swahili)

In Swahili, nouns relating to people often start with the letter *m*: *mtu* (person), *mzee* (old person), *mtoto* (child). When adjectives are applied to these nouns, they also start with an *m* to match the noun: *mtoto mrefu* (tall child), *mtu mzuri* (good person), *mzee mfupi* (short old person).

Mzee — old person (Swahili)

In American culture, it's not considered polite to call someone old, but in Tanzanian culture, age is very important. So calling a man or woman *mzee* is a compliment. Below are two *wazee* (the plural of *mzee*) the author knew in Tanzania.

N'gombe — cow (Swahili)

In Sukuma culture, cows are so important that people sometimes still measure their wealth not by how much land or money they have, but by how many cows they have. In the background of the picture below, a young Tanzanian man keeps an eye on his cattle.

Njia Panda — where the road rises (Swahili)

This village is fictional, but many similar villages existed in Tanzania. The author chose the name deliberately: *njia* (pronounced "n-jee-a") means "road" and *panda* means "rise," so the village name means "where the road rises."

Nyerere, Julius — the first president of Tanzania

Nyerere was elected in 1964, which means Shida would have been about ten at the time. Nyerere was originally a teacher, so people often callen him *Mwalimu*, which means "teacher" in Swahili.

Ny'wadela — a greeting (Sukuma)

Sukuma people say this particular greeting to elders in the afternoon or evening if they haven't greeted their elders earlier that day. Here are some other Sukuma greetings: *ny'wangaluka* (good morning), *ndelagawiza* (good afternoon or evening), *ulemola* (how are you?), and *moleduhu* (I am fine).

Pombe — alcohol (Swahili)

Pombe is a cheap home brew made from cooked and fermented millet.

Shida — problem (Swahili)

This word is pronounced "shee-da," with a long *e*. Unfortunately, as with the main character in this book, *shida* is sometimes used as a name. Parents choose this name if they experience bad luck at the time of their child's birth.

Shikamoo — a greeting given to elders (Swahili)

This greeting literally means "I kiss your feet." The first word children in Tanzania say every morning to their parents and older siblings is *Shikamoo*. Girls bend down on one knee when they say it, as the girl in the picture on the opposite page is doing.

Shing'weng'we monster — a monster from a well-known folk story (Sukuma)

The story of Masala Kulangwa and the Shing'weng'we monster is one of the most famous Sukuma stories. People, especially grandparents, still frequently tell stories in Sukumaland. At the beginning of a story, the listeners all chant "Come, story! Come, story!" and then the storyteller begins by saying "*Zamaaaani*," which means, "A loooong time ago. . . ."

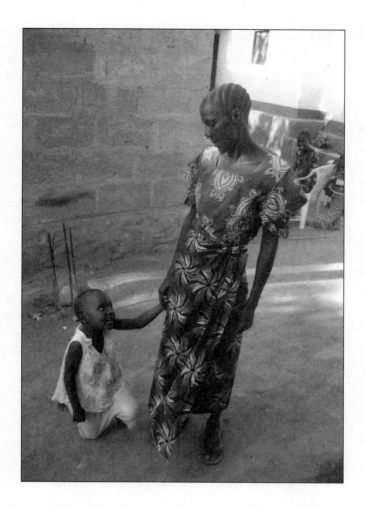

Siafu — army ants (Swahili)

These ants travel in a stream. If a person steps on *siafu*, they'll stream up that person's legs, cover the body, and then start biting. As Gervas shows, the only way to get rid of *siafu* is to take off all your clothes and start pinching the ants off one by one.

Sukuma — a Tanzanian tribe and language

Tanzania has 120 different tribes, and the Sukuma tribe is one of the largest. Sukuma people are originally from Northern Tanzania, around the southern shore of Lake Victoria.

Swahili — the national language of Tanzania

Each tribe in Tanzania has its own language, but Swahili is the national language, spoken between different tribes, at school, on television and radio, and in other public places. Many Tanzanians speak their tribal language at home, Swahili at school, and basic greetings from other tribal languages when they run into friends.

Ugali — a thick porridge (Swahili)

Typically made from maize flour, *ugali* is sticky and pretty tasteless, but most Sukuma people consider it their favorite food because it makes them feel very full. Other popular Sukuma foods include rice, sweet potatoes, and cassava roots. The young woman below is cooking *ugali*.

Uhuru — freedom (Swahili)

People sometimes use *uhuru* to mean independence. Tanzania gained its independence from Britain in 1961, just six years before this story starts, so Shida's people were very proud of their newfound *uhuru*.

Ujamaa — familyhood (Swahili)

President Nyerere appropriated this word to describe his vision of African socialism. His dream was that all Tanzanians would live in *ujamaa* villages where they could share things like farm work, schools, and medical clinics.

Wazungu — people of non-African descent (Swahili)

This word comes from a verb that means to wander aimlessly. When African people met the first European explorers, they gave them this name, thinking perhaps that the explorers were just wandering in circles.

XXXXXXXXXXXXXXX

Photographs in the glossary have been supplied by the author and her Sukuma friend, Modesta Kuzenzia.

Notes from the Author

Why are girls' stories, like Shida's, important?

When I lived in Tanzania, I was struck by how hard Tanzanian girls work. Imagine this: many of them go to school, haul buckets of water on their heads, farm, care for younger siblings, cook food from scratch, scavenge firewood, wash dishes, and mop floors by hand. And then, after all of that, there's still homework! Many girls' school lives are threatened because they lack money for school fees, because teachers threaten to touch their bodies in inappropriate ways, or because the girls are too busy with chores. Being poor is hard work, but being poor and a girl is uniquely challenging.

As you know from our story, over forty years ago President Nyerere spoke about the importance of providing girls equal opportunities. Now many non-profit organizations that work in poor countries say their top priority for improving the world is improving the lives of girls.

If a girl is forced to drop out of school, get married early, and have children, then her children are more likely to be sick and poor, just like her. The cycle of poverty continues. But if a girl is given the opportunity to study as long as she likes — like the nurse in this story — and get married and have babies when and if she wants to, then she'll give all of those gifts back to her community by raising healthy, well-educated, happy kids.

A perfect example is my Sukuma friend Modesta, to whom this book is dedicated. Modesta sold fruit door-to-door to pay for her primary education, but didn't have enough money to go on to secondary school. Poverty made her life challenging. Then someone helped Modesta pay for her education. She finished university, and now Modesta makes Swahili movies and television shows with messages about how to keep people healthy — like how to prevent malaria. She is also paying for her little sister to go to university. In just a few years after completing her education, Modesta has already helped many, many people.

There's a helpful website that talks about some of these ideas. It's **girleffect.org**. Check it out and think about how you can help empower girls (and boys) in your community and around the world.

Did Njia Panda survive as an *ujamaa* village?

Njia Panda is a fictional village, but many like it were set up around Tanzania. President Nyerere had a beautiful dream for his people — that they could work together and share everything: schools, clinics, farms, even machines like tractors. At first, people were invited to join *ujamaa* villages, but eventually they were forced to move to them. This forced relocation made people angry, and the villages tended to make very little money. Eventually President Nyerere had to give up and let people live where they wanted to live.

How is President Nyerere remembered?

Even though President Nyerere's *ujamaa* dream didn't work out, he had a huge impact on his country. During his presidency, people were healthier and lived longer than before, many more kids started attending school (especially girls), and Tanzanians developed a strong sense of national, not just tribal, identity. This sense of national identity is significant when you look at some of the countries that surround Tanzania: Kenya, Uganda, Rwanda, Burundi, and the Democratic Republic of Congo. All of these countries have suffered serious fighting and sometimes civil wars between different tribes, but Tanzania has remained peaceful.

President Nyerere was a uniquely principled leader. When he resigned from his position as president, he moved back to his childhood village and took up farming. When he died, the country shut down for an entire month: people delayed marriages and sporting events, and television and radio stations played only songs of mourning. Pictures of Nyerere's face are still everywhere — on *kitenge*, money, and the walls of public spaces. Tanzanians are still very proud of Nyerere.

Supplemental Online Materials

Visit **katie-quirk.com** and follow the links for *A Girl Called Problem* to find the following resources, and more:

- Author pictures of Tanzania
- A video depicting the life of a modern Tanzanian girl
- Discussion questions for each chapter of the book
- Suggestions for further reading

Acknowledgments

I would like to acknowledge Frans Wijsen and Ralph Tanner for their book, *I Am Just a Sukuma*, which proved critical in my research. I would also like to thank my agent, Sara Crowe, my editor, Kathleen Merz, and the whole team at Eerdmans Books for Young Readers for their wonderful work. Richard Tuschman provided the stunning artwork for the cover, which so beautifully depicts the setting of the novel. I am grateful to Rani, Mo, and Elsa for the childcare they provided so I could work, and to the many generous friends who read and offered feedback on my manuscript. A deep debt of gratitude is owed to Kathryn Reiss at Mills College, Eleanor Vincent, and the other professors and graduate students in whose company I had the privilege of learning for two wonderful years.

My Tanzanian sister, Modesta, taught me many invaluable life lessons while I was in Africa: everything from how to summon up a good Sukuma story, to how to rid a mattress of bedbugs, to how to live gracefully in a world where death and other tragedies are commonplace. I am grateful for my brother, Brian, and for my ever-generous parents, Tim and Sally, for raising me to have such a keen interest in women's and girls' issues, and I am endlessly appreciative of my husband and life partner, Tim, for being such an enthusiastic advocate of my writing and work.

About the Author

Katie Quirk (katie-quirk.com) fell in love with Tanzania, and Sukumaland in particular, when she lived and taught writing on the southern shore of Lake Victoria for two years. Katie currently lives with her family in Maine.